More praise f...
an...

"The narrative is stripped down to a single, inexorable story line that centers on the destructive power of passion. . . . By the end of SIN, all our premonitions of disaster have been alarmingly fulfilled—and they have also been given a particularly horrifying spin. Thanks to Ms. Hart's narrative control, these developments feel both startling and somehow inevitable. . . . The reader looks forward to her next book. Perhaps she will tackle another one of the deadly sins."
—*The New York Times*

"Josephine Hart reprises the hypnotic, doomy tone of *Damage*, fashioning yet another Jezebel for her gallery."
—*New Woman*

"A well-written book . . . There's nothing like the confessions of a sinner to stop us in our tracks."
—*The Denver Post*

"Provocative . . . This fascinating followup to Hart's astonishing debut novel, *Damage*, focuses on the sin of envy. . . . Her compelling voice makes SIN as readable as *Damage*."
—*Library Journal*

Also by Josephine Hart
Published by Ivy Books:

DAMAGE

SIN

Josephine Hart

IVY BOOKS • NEW YORK

Ivy Books
Published by Ballantine Books
Copyright © 1992 by Josephine Hart

Grateful acknowledgement is made to Random House, Inc., and Faber and Faber Limited for permission to reprint an excerpt from ''September 1, 1939'' from *W. H. Auden: Collected Poems* by W. H. Auden, edited by Edward Mendelson. Copyright © 1976 by Edward Mendelson, William Meredith, and Monroe K. Spears, Executors of the Estate of W. H. Auden. Rights outside the U.S. in *Another Time* by W. H. Auden administered by Faber and Faber Limited, London. Reprinted by permission of the publishers.

Library of Congress Catalog Card Number: 92-53853

ISBN 0-8041-1097-2

This edition published by arrangement with Alfred A. Knopf, Inc.

Manufactured in the United States of America

First Ballantine Books Edition: July 1993

To Maurice Saatchi, again

Prologue

There are many ways to have a deprived childhood. One of them is to be too lucky. This knowledge, time's present, comes slowly. They say the veil that hides the future from us was woven by an angel of mercy. But what blinds us to our unpredictable past? Why are we hooded as we search amongst its ruins, trapped in the intricate web of motive and action? Novelists of our own lives, making ourselves up from bits of other people, using the dead and living to tell our tale, we tell tales. This is a tale—fragments from a life. From lives. Particularly mine. And hers.

One

I never knew her really.

I came closest to her through her husband, the man with whom I now live. And through her son, whose name was Stephen.

And through the lie.

There were some, not many, whose world it was natural for me to enter, searching for a secret knowledge of her. And others, peripheral figures, on the outer edges of whose lives I waited, silent, hooded. Hoping to trap some fleeting image that would light my path to her. Whenever I lost her, I slipped under the dark waters of my own life, tracing, from beneath the gloomy waves, the faint white glimmer of her soul. And when she hid from me, I sought her out. For I knew she hid only for advantage later. Subtle, secret, opaque, I would crush her yet.

Though she wounded me beyond pain, I too inflicted deep hurt. Not born to murder her, still I sought to break her. With a small silver hammer of exquisite design, I would seek the exact point at which even the gentlest pressure would smash the glass. And her substance would be mine.

Sometimes, it is in the split-second half decision we nearly didn't make that we stumble by chance into ecstasy, or despair. But chance did not bring her into my life. By grand design she waited for me. In my own home. She was my mother's first child. Though not her firstborn. A terrible injustice to me.

Her name was Elizabeth Ashbridge. And I even envied her that.

Two

❦

"There's something fluttering in my room. Black. Mama, Mama. Something black in my room. Black. With wings. Mama. Mama. Where are you, Mama? Oh please, Mama. Come. Mama. Please. Please. It will land on my face."

I stumble to the door. I cannot reach the light switch. I am too small.

"Mama, I can't. . . . Mama. Mama."

Down the dark corridor. Black.

"Mama. It's coming after me. Oh, Mama. Where are you, Mama?"

I must be near the back stairs. I stretch my arms . . . toes flexed. And still I cannot reach the light. Slowly, rail by rail, I cling to the banisters. And step by step descend into a further darkness.

SIN

The back hall is so narrow. Arms outstretched, I can touch the walls. Wet face . . . stinging thighs . . . little drops of fear and shame.

I stumble onward.

"Mama. Mama." I call towards the blessed light. "Mama."

Her voice, singing softly to the sound of the radio in the background, floats towards me. At last I push the door. Out of the darkness into the light.

And they turn towards me. They are bathed in the light. A perfect trinity. My mother, brush in hand, is seated behind the kneeling Elizabeth. Her golden hair is spread out and down her back. A halo of light. My father, opposite Elizabeth, is bending, almost kneeling, arms outstretched, holding her cocoa.

Perfect happiness. Complete happiness. And I am outside the circle. My mother runs to me. She gathers me in her arms as Elizabeth calls: "Ruth, poor Ruth. You're crying."

My father rises to me, whispering: "Darling Ruth. Darling child. What is it? Oh, you must have come down the back stairs alone in the dark. You poor child."

And they kiss me. They pet me. They hold me. And they try to soothe me.

I am given Elizabeth's cocoa. And Elizabeth kisses me. On my legs.

"Poor, poor Ruth," she whispers.

I start to cry again. Tears of hatred fall on

Elizabeth's head. Onto the golden hair. Then she turns her face up to me. I bend towards her. I brush my face across hers. And a tear drops into her mouth.

Does it sting, Elizabeth? Does it sting?

I am taken up to bed again. Through the main hall, lighted on my way. My mother is cooing as my father now carries me to my room. A search—oh, so thorough—reveals no fluttering object. Just a mobile, half-disconnected from its hook. My father sits with me and strokes my hair, my mother sings her soft song. And I drift off into sleep.

A vision has been burnt into me, a vision of heaven. In darkness, I gaze at the light. The light in which I should have bathed alone.

Three

I believe now that I was exposed too early to goodness and that I never recovered.

Trapped in the fierce grasp of Elizabeth's kindness, aware constantly of the truthfulness of her gaze, I suffocated on the high thinness of the air around her. The corrosive power of her generosity killed, as they rose in me, my own small instincts towards goodness.

It seemed to me that I came wrapped in a caul of darkness and anger into Elizabeth's kingdom. For it was her kingdom. Given to her out of love and pity.

Orphaned at only nine months, she was the child of my mother's sister, Astrid, and of Oliver Ord Ashbridge, young, married lovers killed in a car crash. Elizabeth was taken to Lexington. Its old walls wove a stone sanctuary round her, and its famous gardens and lake gave to all her freedoms a restricted, formal beauty. So she lived in Lexington, loved and cherished, a daughter for my parents. Before me.

Except, I was their only daughter. A blood right. One they had taken from me.

No one was to blame. They had done what was right and good. They had given a home to Elizabeth. My home. And left me with the pain of something irretrievable, lost.

I would be forever, falsely the second. Not only the second, but one of a pair: less valuable without the other.

My mother and father were oblivious to the effect on me of their careful, equal love. On my mind's eye they painted pictures for me. Of love and gentleness. Pictures that I came to hate: my mother sighing during the careful plaiting of Elizabeth's long, blond hair—which took more time than the vigorous brushing of my short, black curls. "There is a solution, Mama," I wanted to cry. "Cut Elizabeth's hair. Throw it away. Burn it." But I said nothing. For in those days I learned patience. Slow, hidden patience.

My father, kneeling again, before Elizabeth, as she sat sobbing on her bed, on the day she left for boarding school. Patting her hand to comfort her and whispering, "Oh, my golden girl. My golden light."

Stop painting these pictures for me, my heart cried. Stop. "You've never knelt to me, Papa. You've never knelt to me. She's not yours, Papa. She's not yours."

They didn't stop.

Still I see the sad way they gazed at me in the week after she left—when I copied little things I'd seen her do, that had elicited praise. And I hear them sighing, "Ah, you miss her too, Ruth. I know, my dear. I know."

I see my mother, seated in front of the head-mistress's desk, pleading with her to put us in the same house—a practice normally frowned upon at the school. "It's essential to keep them close. Less lonely, for Ruth, who depends on Elizabeth so."

Two girls made my parents happy. Elizabeth and Ruth, the one following the other, made the magic.

A magic that Elizabeth created. Encouraged when small to follow the sweetness of her behaviour—to imitate her many acts of generosity, to note her kindness—I followed in cold envy the path she laid before me through the years. Like Satan before the Fall, I came to hate the very nature of goodness, to fear its power.

But during childhood I lacked the courage for rebellion. So I went underground. To search for secret ways to be. And secret ways to lessen her.

Sometimes, as directed, I took her behaviour. And copied it. Then . . . her things. And hid them. Childish things for childish times. Her mug, the

9

one with the red rabbits. Her favourite doll. The rag dog with the yellow mouth. Ribbons. I smiled to watch her search for them. And once to see her weep. For the doll.

I used her smile. Sometimes. It didn't suit.

Later, as adolescence stole upon us at our boarding school, I built a different, though still small, collection. Underwear. Hair slides. Stockings. Insignificant items. Rarely used, always in secret.

In those years of fierce discovery sometimes I would reach for myself and sigh. And often bank it down for a later conflagration.

And so it all began in small ways. Maybe it always does. Small thefts. Little meannesses. Malicious pleasures. Minor cruelties.

But what if I had been there before Elizabeth? What if I had been born first? Would she have been . . . like me? What if Seth, the third son after Cain and Abel, had been firstborn? What if the Lord had been pleased by Cain's gift? Would Cain ever have disturbed the sleeping monster in himself?

I chose my habit. I had, you understand, no grand schemes. For I was not ambitious. I did not need public applause. I was spiritual by nature. A spiritual, malevolent creature. There are, I believe, many of us about.

Four

I was never promiscuous. I chose my lovers with intelligence and, I believe, some originality. Though my victims were players on a board of my design, even my arbitrary, predatory swoops were accomplished with some artistry.

I am beautiful. A statement of fact. A statement of power. I have dark hair and sallow, almost poreless skin. My deep-set brown eyes slant slightly upwards. My eyebrows—and this is much commented upon—do not arch, but seem to wing themselves across my brow. My nose is long, narrow and straight. My mouth is strong, and even without lipstick my lips are red. It is a face in which the regularity of my features is made slightly exotic by the intensity of my colouring. "She's a di Malta,"

11

my mother had often commented—referring to my father's Italian mother. I am of above average height, in fact only slightly less tall than Elizabeth. I have, however, a voluptuous figure.

Physically, therefore, I was well equipped for the arena. But, most crucially for my future success, I had what amounted to genius in my deep knowingness of the beat, of the pounding rhythm of desire.

As a young woman I had, of course, a different assemblage of Elizabeth's things. A small collection. Silk underwear now. Hair adornments, two of them gold. Lipstick. Shoes, high heeled, black. Other insignificant items. I still used them rarely, and still always in secret.

After Oxford, where I read English, I joined a small book publishing house as an editorial assistant. I progressed steadily, as careful in hiding my wealth as I was subtle in the deployment of my beauty.

Like all truly beautiful women I dressed with extreme simplicity. I was aware that to emphasise for dramatic effect my already exotic colouring, or to shape clothes around the full curves of my body, would be to court vulgarity. Also it would rob me of the element of surprise, and undermine the precepts of stealth which are so essential to the successful disarming of prey.

I had a small wardrobe of simple, elegant dresses—usually navy or white in the summer, and a soft cream (to which I am rather attached) and black in the winter, occasionally lifted by a touch of red. My accessories were extremely expensive and always in perfect condition. But the classic nature of their design, and the comparative dullness of their colour, deflected attention from the fact that my handbags, for example, could cost over a month's salary.

This particular method of presentation reassured my female colleagues. The men I met at work soon found that their advances towards me elicited a response of such vague elusiveness that—initially attracted by the mysterious quality surrounding me—they eventually retreated. Baffled, but with their pride still in place.

Though my colleagues were not aware of it, and indeed the idea was only half-formed, I considered the possibility of trying to build a small book publishing division within my father's magazine empire. I had a lot to learn.

In London, I lived during the week in an elegant flat in a cul-de-sac behind Harrods. It was discreet. Though clearly implying that I did not live on my salary alone, it avoided any overt statement of my financial position. From this base I pursued a social life that, by careful manipulation, ran parallel to that of Elizabeth. I believed myself to be in control.

Elizabeth was striking. Not beautiful. The promise of those early childhood years of golden hair and fine features had faded into a pale attractiveness, that she seemed unwilling to redeem in any way. It was her height, inherited from her father, Oliver, that made an impact. She was long-limbed, and slender. Her shoulders were of a slightly masculine strength, which the severity of her clothes seemed to emphasise.

If mine was a wardrobe picked with care for a purpose only I could comprehend, hers seemed to be genuinely the result of a fastidious cleanliness, a high purity, that almost festered the eye. She dressed in white shirts of cotton or silk, with jeans or tailored trousers. In the evening, she wore velvet or silk jackets over longish, silk skirts, which she seemed to wrap sarong-like around her long waist. During the day, her hair was worn back from her face and held by a barrette. In the evening it was pleated into a simple chignon. It was a style that remained unchanged through the years as almost identical new items replaced the old.

After art school—where Elizabeth enjoyed a modest success—she lived in an enormous studio flat in Kensington, where she painted. Obsessed with sky, she was unfashionable, rarely exhibited and in my opinion totally without talent.

Her friends were few, and mostly artists. However, she retained from her school days a close relationship with the Baathus family, respected international bankers. Maria Baathus regularly invited Elizabeth to Paris, and to the Loire, where

the family had a château. Elizabeth accepted those
invitations with almost child-like joy. This hos-
pitality she returned, by inviting Maria Baathus
for occasional visits to Lexington. These visits
were much appreciated by Maria, who seemed to
love Lexington and its famous lake. For its "mystery," she'd once said.

Lexington is, from one perspective, a hidden,
secret house. It is approached by a winding, climb-
ing drive through woods. Then a sudden clearing
and, shockingly, Lexington, washed red, com-
mands the hill. Long, open parkland falls gently
through tree-shadowed acres into water-light.

Lexington, the house and lake into which over
time we poured so much of our lives, had been
acquired by my grandfather in the first flush of his
spectacular business success. "The ultimate chess
game," as he described it.

He had bought a small magazine publishing
company with well-established, though not very
profitable, titles. He moved the company out of its
enormous, old-fashioned building in central London, and thereby realised the hidden asset he had
seen all along. The property. With a considerable
fortune in the bank from the sale of the building,
within three years he had closed six weak magazines, transformed others into market leaders and
successfully launched two more. He had created a
publishing empire—Alpha Publishing. So called
because my grandmother's name was Alexa, and

Josephine Hart

they had called their two daughters Astrid and
Aileen. "All Alphas" had been his little joke.

After her husband died, my grandmother, either
from grief or from joy, had Lexington's grey stone
washed red.

My grandfather and my father returned from
London each weekend and pursued male pastimes
of fishing, hunting, cards. Weekends at Lexington
were full of male odours, of an alien pitch of
laughter that as a child had thrilled me. Even the
colour of Lexington had seemed to change—its red
hue seemed daring and triumphant. During its female week it had seemed to me blood red, with
black somewhere clotted in its depths.

Five

I have never been interested in handsome men. This is not because I believe that they are necessarily vain; nor indeed that they are incapable, as is often implied, of loving deeply. No. I know that nature is not all-bountiful, and, having endowed beauty, it will almost certainly not feel the necessity to be generous with other qualities.

On a summer's day when Elizabeth was in her late twenties, into Lexington walked the reason for the increased frequency of her visits to France. Hubert Baathus.

He strode across the lawn towards my garden chair, his smiling, courtly face a veritable topography of the balances and planes of light and shade that make a man handsome.

It is true that it was with a minimum of originality I intended on the seduction of Elizabeth's lover, a plan conceived in the split second of his arrival. This banality did not, would not in any way, lessen the pain she would suffer.

I smiled at him through the sunlight, and held my hand out for his perfect bow. And for the kiss on the hand, which, as he was a gentleman, avoided final contact.

"Elizabeth speaks of you with such admiration—I have so longed to meet you."

"You're too kind," I replied.

"Too kind? Can one ever be too kind?"

My too clever weekend guest, Helen, now spoke.

"You're taking the phrase too literally, Hubert. Sometimes in England we say, 'you're too kind,' and mean something entirely different."

Hubert looked at me slightly puzzled.

"I am sure I got Ruth's meaning correctly. How clumsy I sound. My English is . . . stilted."

"No. Your English is charming," I said.

"Ah, yes. Charming. Now I do understand what the English mean when they say 'charming.' I understand the 'nuance.' "

He laughed. Elizabeth smiled gently at his little triumph.

"Hubert may come to live in London for three or four years," she said.

"Really? Why?" I asked.

"We have established a branch of the Bank in London. I will stay for a time to develop it before returning to Paris."

"Do you think you'll like living in England?"

"Oh yes. I am certain of that." He shot a look of affection towards Elizabeth.

"Have you ever lived in London before?" I asked.

"Lived, no. But I have visited often. I love London. Its theatre particularly . . . is the best in the world. But now I seem to flatter you, no?"

"We like being flattered."

Helen was now smiling at him too. Her cleverness had been put to one side as an inappropriate accessory in the face of his charm.

Elizabeth was entranced. But why did she interest him? Did he perhaps have a lust for her soul? What a potent weapon it is when observed with the clarity of vision required to appreciate it. How serious were they about each other? Elizabeth? Very. Hubert?

"Ruth."

Startled, I turned towards my mother.

"Ruth, dear. You seem lost in thought. We should move to the terrace, darling. Lunch is ready."

I watched Elizabeth and Hubert walk towards the house. He had his arm about her waist, and she turned towards him. And gazed at him as if to light his path. Even on a summer day.

I walked after them. My shadow fell across

them. They stopped, and turned to me, smiling. I placed myself on the other side of Hubert.

"I hope we'll see you at Lexington at the weekends when you come to live in England."

"Hubert starts next month," Elizabeth said.

"You've bought somewhere to live in London?"

"No. There is a company flat. In Mayfair. I shall stay there, at least for the immediate future."

We had arrived at the house. Lunch was being served on the terrace. Folds of white linen—an obsession of my mother, whose linen cupboard had an almost Alpine purity—fell from the oblong table onto the grey stone of the terrace. I watched Hubert eat. He was full of appetite, but discreet. An interesting tension. Elizabeth smiled with pleasure as he complimented my father on the wine—which he drank in considerable quantities, though not to excess. He goes just to the edge, I thought. But no further.

Elizabeth toyed with her food. She drank virtually nothing. Elizabeth never goes to the edge. In her painting, for example, there is no danger, no excitement. As if he had read my thoughts, Hubert spoke.

"I admire Elizabeth's painting very much. She is committed to beauty. She is very much in the French tradition. We do not celebrate . . . ugliness . . . just because it shocks. You understand?" He turned to me.

"Yes, indeed I do." I tried to sound diplomatic. "But great art has always shocked. N'est-ce pas?"

"Yes. But Elizabeth does not claim to be a great artist, Ruth. She does, however, have a true eye.

And in time she may surprise you all. I have a feeling about . . ."

"Oh, Hubert. Please." Blushing, Elizabeth interjected. "It's simple really. Painting is all I'm good at. And even at that, I have only a small talent. But it makes me very happy, and my small successes encourage me to continue with my . . ."

"Enchantment?" Hubert offered.

"Well!" sighed Helen. "You make an enchanted couple. God knows there aren't many around."

"Ruth, where's Dominick?" asked my mother. When he was not asking me to marry him, I found Dominick useful company on occasional weekends at Lexington.

"He's in America, Mother. Giving a series of lectures at Berkeley," I replied.

Dominick's subject, mathematics, was such that it rendered any conversation concerning his work impossible. All enquiries were full of dread—that he might be tempted to explain. He read modern novels, avidly. Most of them he loathed. "It gives me something to talk about," he often said laughingly.

Yes, he had his charms. But with me he had strayed onto the wrong path. One of these days I would have to lead him to an exit. I hoped that he would leave with grace.

Six

"Ruth."

"Elizabeth."

"I don't deserve this, Ruth."

I smiled briefly back at her.

"I don't deserve to be so happy. From the moment I saw him . . ."

"I'm sure he feels the same. Like Dante and Beatrice. 'I did but see her passing by and yet will love her till I die.' "

"You always have the right words, Ruth. Always. It's such a gift."

And her radiance—the bride's radiance, caught in the long, oval mirror—seemed fairy-tale. Unreal. As though the images were such a powerful distillation of reality that finally only the image

existed. I moved behind her, my deep rose dress
blotted out by the folds of ivory in which Elizabeth stood. She turned suddenly. For a second we
stood eye to eye. The bride and her maid of honour. She kissed me. I made no move. What should
I betray? And, with the touch of Elizabeth's cool
lips still seeming to flutter on my cheek, I followed
her from her room to join my mother in the hall.

"Oh, Elizabeth. You look beautiful."

"Mother." Elizabeth embraced her.

Mother. Not true. And shortly after, *Father.* Not
true either. His turn to worship. Then steadily,
past various acolytes, we made our way through
Elizabeth's enchanted time to the church, and to
Hubert.

It is indeed a holy thing, the ritual of marriage.
I looked at Hubert. His features had a kind of classic timelessness. It would ensure that any photo-
graph of him stumbled upon in a trunk, or in a
corner of some room, by an adolescent girl in time
to come would elicit a little gasp of appreciation—
that men could be so beautiful. As he turned towards Elizabeth, his face witnessed truth and love.
I felt no pain. They should love each other . . . I
searched for a word . . . profoundly. That was satisfying to me. Its perfection challenged me. Why
mar something already imperfect? It is the first
crack that ruins the Ming. The first lie that de-
stroys Truth. The first adultery that breaks the
conjunction. After that it's only repetition.

And after that, of course, it is always repetition. When perfection is defiled it is hard to resist the pleasures of destruction, and of lies, and of concupiscence. For then the sacrifice is for nothing.

And so I stood, rose-coloured, beside the lily, and examined quietly the tiny thorns of my bouquet.

I walked behind them, down the aisle. Alone. The third. Hooded, in silk. Then other rosy maidens followed us out into the low, gold summer day, which spread its slightly cloying warmth around the marble purity of the newly wedded couple.

Lexington, as though drunk, seemed to dance with the rhythm of their laughter and to twinkle back at each and every smile. Long tables in the courtyard followed the shape of the house. The principal table was centred before the main building for the key actors in the tableau. Two long tables, on either side, followed the shape of the east and west wings of Alexa's old dynastic dream for her daughters. After lunch and speeches, people drifted dreamily down the lawns, and a few towards the greater privacy of the distant lake.

"They make a perfect couple." Charlotte Baathus, Hubert's twin sister, spoke to me.

"Oh. Yes, indeed. Perfect."

"It was so sudden," she said.

"Yes."

"I will admit I was a little . . . surprised. Shocked

even. Though Maria is thrilled. Maria always adored Elizabeth."

"Shocked? Why shocked?"

"Well," she went on. "They decided to marry within a month of Hubert coming to London. Then the wedding was so . . . soon . . . after that."

"Elizabeth wanted a summer wedding. There seemed no point in waiting until next summer," I replied.

I disliked Charlotte Baathus. Whereas Hubert was handsome, she had the common prettiness of the pale-blue-eyes-and-rosy-lips kind. She had a soft, rather breathless way of speaking her almost accentless English.

"Charlotte," I said. "I wasn't at all shocked by the speed of the announcement. They are"—the word came again—"profoundly, in love."

"Oh, yes," she said. I saw that she did not like the idea. To a trained observer like myself, it takes the merest tightening of the muscles round the mouth to show the meanness of the soul.

I kissed Charlotte briefly. I hoped the kiss confused her, coming so soon after my tiny victory. I enjoyed the slight tension of her arm muscles, as I held them before the predatory swoop of my lips, which was impossible for her to escape.

I walked away, and found another group of contented witnesses to Elizabeth's and Hubert's joy. I agreed wholeheartedly with excessive tributes to her beauty. I listened to some friends of Elizabeth, describing with seeming honesty her endless kindness to them. And I thought of how their sudden decision to marry had turned my plan into something much more interesting, more dangerous and more difficult.

With soft smiles, I approached a hopeful Dominick. And I marvelled again at what a secret thing the human heart is, and the human mind. A merciful protection for us all. For who would survive a journey round the mind of another?

No one in the world—no one knew my thoughts. God? I wondered idly. Did God know? Or knowing, care?

Seven

A mathematician in love does not approach his beloved with a scientific analysis of the laws of probability of relationships. Particularly a mathematician whose love is not returned.

But perhaps there is a scientific law here after all. Does the love of the lover expand or contract in direct relation to the love returned or withheld? Who can fail to believe that the intensity of one's adoration, if further developed, will not elicit a response? "If there is love in this heart," the saying goes, "then there is love in that heart. For one hand claps not without the other." How seductive. And how wrong. For why trap what is already trapped? It is only in flight that we know the freedom of the bird.

These were my idle thoughts on a walk with Dominick after the wedding. Thoughts concealed by my soft smile at his protestations, and expectations. For Dominick had developed the habit of expectation.

And this being a light, feather-soft day, and our being hidden on the other side of the lake, his attempts at seduction were successful. His expectations were fulfilled.

My decision. I allowed. I deigned. It was essential with Dominick to keep a distance. I knew it, he did not. I watched through shuttered eyes his disintegration. And into the after-minutes, while his body reassembled itself, I dreamed a little dream of Elizabeth and Hubert. Their conjunction—in holy matrimony. And again I felt no pain. Dominick whispered words of marriage again into my closed heart. With a sigh of irritation I left my thoughts. I planted doubt, and then its cruel cousin hope, in his heart. But not rejection. I had chosen to lay down my head on the quilted heart of a hosta, crushing it. I felt no guilt. Nature, after all, has never loved us back.

We two walked back to Lexington, its guests now gone. A liar and her lad, with his clever, modish face. His straw-coloured hair endlessly flopping into his glasses. His long body, and all its lines that did not entrance me.

We sat around the table with my mother and father. We ate tiny grilled fish. Then cold chicken covered in a pale lemon cream, and decorated with black olives shaped into hearts. The lilies on the table, some with the closed heads of snakes, gently opened during dinner. Predator turned victim.

I drank red wine and wondered idly what Elizabeth and Hubert were doing. Now. Exactly now. In my mind's eye, I wandered up and down her familiar body. I tried to imagine it with Hubert's eye. And thought of that secret event, for which we find private places, hidden rooms, or darkness. So that no one else will see the particular way man and woman become one. Man thrusting blindly upwards, through the same passage that once he blindly travelled down into the world. Believing that he brings pleasure where once there had been pain. But still it leads to defeat. For from that sweetness come the pain and blood again, as down the passage the cranium pushes through bone. Again. And never once does God ask us for forgiveness.

The red wine in my stomach sickened me. And, idiotically shocked, I thought of Elizabeth pregnant. In birth. A mother.

"They will be very happy together." My father spoke.

"Is that an order?" I asked.

"Ruth, dear. It's simply my assessment."

"Based, dear Father, on exactly what?"

"On my knowledge that a man would be foolish indeed not to be happy with Elizabeth."

"Ah. She has a secret formula, does she? Perhaps when she returns from Greece she can explain it to Dominick. Then he can create a mathematical formula for happiness and become famous. The Dominick Garton Principle of Happiness in Marriage, based on the Ashbridge-Baathus model. First discovered in the Greek archipelago while the couple were on honeymoon."

Before my father could voice his disapproval, I blew him a kiss, and said: "It's a joke, Father. A joke. Of course they'll be gloriously happy together. And you're right. What man could fail to love Elizabeth?"

My father and mother smiled at each other in uncertain relief.

"And what man could fail to be happy with you, Ruth?" Dominick blew me a kiss.

"Ah, Dominick. My only fan. I do not see myself built for happiness. It's almost an alien concept to me."

"What nonsense, Ruth. What utter nonsense," said my father.

"Non sense. Only to you, Father. It makes sense to me."

"You've had a wonderfully happy life so far. Don't be so careless of it. Let's look at the facts."

My father and I had often engaged in this semi-banter. It was our own language barrier. It had a certain style, specific rules, and achieved the overall objective—non-communication. An essential between adult child and parent. His legal training naturally led him to believe that a question-and-answer technique was the road to the truth. He always forgot that I was not under oath.

"I'm going back to the flat tonight." Dominick rose to go. "I have an early lecture in the morning."

"Elizabeth mentioned last week that she is going to keep her studio," my mother said.

"Yes. She's decided to go on painting there. Hubert's flat is too small," replied Dominick.

Dominick lived in the same block of flats as Elizabeth. A mathematician with an artist's studio flat. This gave him, he believed, the bohemian air he rather longed for. His was an intelligence trapped within the wrong temperament. But such was his brilliance, and so quickly had it been recognised and rewarded by schools and universities, that the wunderkind never had a chance. He was later so loaded down with academic achievement that he was forced to succumb, and he became his talent. Almost to the same degree as he became English.

His parents were American. His father, like Dominick, was a noted mathematician. His mother, after a number of years at the Massachusetts Institute of Technology, had become a senior consultant to McKinsey.

During a carefully planned mutual assignment to London, he to the London School of Economics, she to the London office of the parent company, Dominick attended Westminster School. There, he fell in love with England. And with all things English. He believed his passion was reciprocated—a familiar blindness in Dominick.

Later, after his parents returned to America, he decided on Trinity College, Cambridge, as opposed to Harvard. There he began to accept what he had only half-understood at Westminster, that his passionate seriousness about his work needed to be leavened by irony. And that, in polite society in England, the sciences were rarely to be mentioned. A minor flirtation with the arts was much more laudable.

I met him at a little party Elizabeth had given a few years previously. As visits to his flat would provide me with a perfect lookout, I encouraged his interest. My seduction of Dominick, in both strategy and tactics, was so subtly planned and executed that in the moment of possession it was his face which portrayed triumph. The increasing urgency of his deepening love for me was the only complication in an otherwise perfect scenario.

Before Dominick there had, of course, been men. There was an early boyfriend of Elizabeth's—a Mexican painter who, to my disappointment (I found this out too late), she had rejected. Then there was a liaison with a wholly unsuitable member of the aristocracy who was playing with the idea of being an artist. That . . . romance . . . had allowed me a stolen weekend in Paris. And that side of himself which I guessed he had kept well hidden from Elizabeth was allowed full rein. An interesting and educational two days. The son of a Lexington neighbour proved a much duller conquest. His guilt at his betrayal of Elizabeth was so excessive as to be almost amusing.

I looked at Dominick. Ruth's dedicated lover, never Elizabeth's. The decision to keep her studio surprised me. Elizabeth hadn't told me—perhaps believing it to be of no consequence. But it was of great consequence for Dominick. I sighed. For the immediate future at least, it rather seemed as if Dominick, and our relationship, would survive.

Eight

"Well, you two . . . you couple."

Hubert smiled. He and Elizabeth, Dominick and I were having a welcome-home dinner at a restaurant close to their home. Elizabeth was not a cook.

Bronzed, hair bleached, dressed in cream silk shirt and dark brown skirt, Elizabeth talked of Greece. Each word was shot through with love. She spoke of colour with her pretty painter's eye, and I felt sure that inevitably she had entered her Greek period. Its blue-green lightness and celestial white would be broken only by some cascade of blushing pink petals. Or perhaps, for dramatic contrast, a black-clothed peasant would ride or stride his or her way across the canvas.

"Well, Madame et Monsieur Hubert Baathus,

newly wed . . . happily married . . . give us a definition of married happiness." Dominick was always searching for definitions.

"It does not exist," Hubert said.

Elizabeth looked shocked.

"Marriage has no intrinsic happiness. Happiness
is to be with the one. And to be the only one for
the other."

"With or without marriage?"

"Yes. Though the ease and convenience and
pleasure of formal togetherness is a delightful
thing. A wise thing. So marriage is wise happiness.
No?"

"Your English is improving dramatically."

"Thank you, Ruth." He smiled at me.

"Hubert's English is only a little stilted when he
first meets people. He is shy." Elizabeth spoke.

"Shy? . . . Only a little," I replied.

"Wise happiness. I really like that. You both, I
hope, will have years and years of wise happiness." Dominick raised his glass. "To wise happiness—the happiness of Elizabeth and Hubert."

We all went back to Hubert's flat, now their
home, for coffee. It was a masculine flat, heavy,
dark woods, paisley-patterned curtains, leather sofas—conventional, though elegant. The handsome
abode of a handsome man. He looked at me looking at the flat.

"We'll move to Paris in a couple of years. It

seemed pointless to set about furnishing a new house."

"Is that definite?" Dominick asked. I was still digesting the thought of separation.

"Oh yes," replied Hubert.

"That's why I'll continue to paint in my studio, until we go to Paris," Elizabeth added. "Hubert assures me that I will have a studio, high at the top of the house."

I envisaged a new Paris period of rooftops—grey-slated. Which cliché would she pick? Wise happiness was, I felt, going to be very boring. But if I were Elizabeth, what would I find with Hubert? If I were Elizabeth?

"Well, we must leave you two. It's a joy to see you back again. So harmonious. I'm always searching for mathematical harmonies—their beauty would astound you. The Greeks believed they were the essence of goodness, you know."

"Why, Dominick. I've never heard you speak so romantically about your work before."

"No, Ruth. Perhaps I'm afraid of mockery." He did not say whose.

"Love's a miracle. A way of seeing someone . . . suffused by light. It's like my painting, my un-fashionable, light-filled painting. Love's an extra dimension to sight. It gives a light that only the loved one seems to have. And only the lover sees. That's how I see . . . Hubert."

Elizabeth turned away at the end of her extraor-

dinary little speech. A speech quite out of character. In her thin, fine face there was a frightening
fierceness. Had I, through my astonishment, betrayed my hatred? Had she run for cover?

"Previously, my life was a little spoiled and
selfish. Elizabeth has made me better." Hubert,
handsome, happy—and humble.

"And what is the outward sign of this improve-
ment?" I tried to sound mocking.

"There's no outward sign, Ruth. But I have
changed. For example, I mock less."

I had been put in my place.

"Well, Hubert, your English has certainly im-
proved. No problem with nuance anymore."

He laughed.

"Oh, Ruth, you too will melt."

Dominick winced at this implication that he was
ineffective in thawing my coldness.

Sensitive as ever, Elizabeth noticed. "Dominick
has, I think, already started the process. Now I'll
be very French, and give you two kisses and say
au revoir."

The kisses were perfunctory. We waved goodbye, and left. The less harmonious couple.

Nine

Is it possible to seduce a happily married man in the early days of his marriage? Particularly a man who sees in his new wife qualities that have meant little to him before.

The ordinary strategies would most certainly not work. Swimming too close to him in the discreetly hidden pool at Lexington, or over-enthusiastically leaning forward in low-cut gown, which I rarely wore anyway. Such full frontal assaults were not for such as he.

At a celebration dinner for my parents' anniversary I wore a perfect curve of dark, red velvet. Though it served to emphasise the ripeness of my body, I knew the effect to be of little interest from the lack of tension in his open, smiling response.

And, to be truthful, I too disdained the slight vulgarity of my display.

No, Elizabeth had not married a fool. And the light she saw around him allowed no access. Slowly I began to accept that, with Hubert, perhaps only patient malevolence might work.

There was a day—at Lexington. We sat together in the garden. Alone, for some reason. And I tried to hold him with my eyes. I moved—subtly—closer to him. He looked at me. Coldly. Knowingly? Then he stood up. "I think I can see Elizabeth. Excuse me, Ruth."

Was there an ambivalence? In the words? Or had I been given a signal? "Keep a distance." Had he absorbed me, Ruth? Or simply recognised my purpose?

Sometime after that I suffered a mild illness. When I left the hospital I felt weary. And as Dominick persisted with his entreaties, I thought of surrender. To him. In marriage. Why not?

My secret life, with its thrilling labyrinthine ways and fierce cacophony of voices—my own surface voice, its contradictory echo and the imagined voice of my victim—enthralled but increasingly weakened me.

My work, never the centre, became more and more peripheral. "Making my way" in publishing was neither necessary to me financially nor of profound interest to me intellectually. I had proved to myself that I had the ability and the discipline to succeed in my chosen field. My life's ambition, however, lay elsewhere.

And Dominick was, in his way, appealing. I enjoyed his adoration. He was totally within my control. The idea, once considered, grew more powerful. And Dominick, sensing victory, made a sudden assault of great intensity. Flattered, and not a little exhausted, I succumbed.

We were married quietly in London. Lexington had already had its triumphant wedding day. I did not want to be the second bride.

But later I was again pre-empted. Elizabeth became pregnant. Her son, Stephen, born after a cesarean operation, brought extraordinary joy to both Elizabeth and Hubert. Their flat was reorganised for the new baby, and Hubert's return to Paris was postponed. The proud father—the happy husband—remained pure.

And Stephen became a catalyst for William, who was born almost two years later by easy vaginal delivery—a son for me and for Dominick. Now Dominick had everything he wanted. The woman he loved, and a son. Is it any wonder that I sometimes sought to punish him?

I was, however, a good mother. A dedicated mother. When I looked at William I ceased to think. I discovered in myself a desire to worship. Porcelain perfection, bathed by me and then dressed again. The impenetrable mystery of cries

and silences, and eyes that gazed back in flat
knowingness.

Later, a tough, sturdy mobility, moving towards me. Then, old sounds made new. Mostly
for me. Surely it should have been enough. For
me. For anyone. But then it never has been.

When the maternity nurse left, everything to do
with William was done by me. Dominick was both
surprised and elated by this.

I knew my love for William entranced him. So
there was solace for Dominick. I kept a balance
for him. It seemed only fair.

Having bought the adjacent studio flat, with
great care to maintain his beloved harmony of di-
mensions, Dominick created a space of order and
symmetry for his beautiful wife and child.

Against a backdrop of white walls, he placed, in
careful patterns, a geometry of furniture. At an-
gles, touching, cream chaises-longues, a circle of
black chairs, a perfect rectangle of low wooden
tables with wrought-iron legs—old Indian tables,
he told me. An antique globe dominated one end
of the living room and a magnificent telescope
stood at the other.

William's room was small, buttercup yellow. On
his bed, impossibly coloured green cows and
shepherds seemed to chase each other through a
yellow field of flowers. He found them soothing,
and grasped his soft cover to him like a rag-doll
lover, one who offers no resistance.

Our bedroom was a subtle contrast of blues and navy. Dominick created, behind a hidden door—I have a key—a long walk-in dressing room for me. Along one side, on racks, were the clothes that wrapped round the body Dominick adored. My shoes stood in neat, colour-coded battalions. On open shelves, my carefully folded sweaters sat softly, one on top of the other, an organised rainbow of black and cream and red. A small dressing table contained a pretty array of creams and powders—less attractive objects remained in their drawers.

It was here, in this narrow, dark room that I kept the items belonging to Elizabeth. The high heels—black patent. Two silk slips—one olive green, one black—to which I had made some alterations, to suit the different requirements of my body. Stockings. A hairbrush, a new acquisition. A beret. Also new.

I was aware of the sexual connotations of many of these items and of the purpose to which I might put them. However, even these most intimate accoutrements did not imply a lust for Elizabeth's body. No, I was much more demanding. Elizabeth never seemed to miss these items. Would you? Such small things? Over years?

Initially, in the early days of my marriage, I was very secretive—hiding them under layers of clothes. Or placing them, with care, at the back of drawers. But as time passed, my dressing room became more and more my private domain, never to be invaded. I relaxed. These "items" were not for normal wear.

They were for secret times. Times when I gazed in fascination at my Elizabeth-decorated body and walked around my dark kingdom in a kind of trance.

The pattern of my early relationship with Dominick continued in marriage. I became increasingly fascinated by my power over him. It was, I knew, a small achievement. A small art. But then I was never ambitious. Few people are. Perhaps there is in us some inherited, ancient knowledge. The majority do not desire the world—knowing on some primitive level that it disappoints. They are quite content to let the blind few pursue their path to wisdom. And to watch those trapped by genius forced to sacrifice themselves, and those trapped by talent to emulate them. Much better to be in the audience, watching the actors find the surprise ending.

Ten

Perhaps I was numbed by motherhood. I moved through time, as though in a fog. And five years slumbered on to the telephone call.

A call to Lexington, where Elizabeth and I, our husbands both away on business, had decided to spend the weekend.

I took the call. I listened. Then I carefully put down the receiver. I stayed for a long time, alone, in the sitting room. Then finally and very slowly I went to find her. She was cutting roses in the garden.

She turned and saw my face. Something told her to run away from me. From the terrace she ran across the lawn. Half-walking, half-running through parkland, she stumbled through the bushes and staggered on and on towards the lake. Trying to escape from the knowledge I had. The knowledge I would bring to her. When I caught her. Or when she stopped. Which would happen sooner? It was a question of courage. Hers.

And of course finally, magnificent, she turned to me.

I whispered the words.

"No. *No.*" She screamed.

And she fell—the body's truth in the great moments of life.

Of all those who could have brought her such a truth, I was the messenger. Selected by chance—Dominick's trip to California; my parents' visit to London. I stood and watched her as the knowledge wound itself around her. And I listened, as she made the high, thin sounds of a woman mourning. Razor-sharp sounds that cut the air.

And then, on her knees still, she beat the ground for him. But it resisted. Or if it softened at all, it was only to receive him later.

She was defeated. A defeat so instant, so total, that her past life died in a second. And her new one came screamingly alive. She was stunned alive by an expert, and death had taken her protection away. I saw it all in a second's pitiless pity. Then, I knelt beside her and comforted the tragic widow. And I thought that I would never break them now. Or ever know her through Hubert. In a sense I had been robbed of my prey.

Eleven

We bury with many different emotions. Rarely with intimations of mortality. "Buried" is the ultimate separation of them and us. As others' lives are often only dreams to us, so also others' deaths.

Only occasionally is there agony. And it was Elizabeth's that day. Grief swelled her face as though all the fluids of the body, lymph and blood, were surging in a wave of revolt, crashing against the rocks of bone structure. Her eyes, however, remained abnormally still.

It seemed excessive to me. But I could feel its power. I kept my distance.

I thought of a year hence, or perhaps five years. Hubert, a dreamy ghost of a handsome husband—a memory to be respected by the second husband.

For he would most assuredly arrive, from somewhere in the future. To live the life Hubert had lost. Would it make a difference? To her? In five years' time?

After the Latin mass, and the searing Dies Irae, Elizabeth—my father's hand firmly on her elbow, and followed immediately by Hubert's parents, tall, trembling, not touching each other—led the procession down the aisle of the seventeenth-century chapel in Tours. I walked, profoundly calm, beside my weeping mother. Dominick was not with me. He had, sensibly and kindly, taken a bewildered Stephen and an excited William to friends in Scotland.

The English mourners whispered as they followed the cortege to the small cemetery where Hubert was to join his ancestors.

"Modern plague, car crashes. Biggest killer of men under . . ."

"No one else was killed. That was a mercy."

"It took hours to get him out—he was badly . . ."

"He was terribly . . . broken. Everything." The Frenchman searched for words. "Everything . . . broken . . ."

Except the eyes. Which of course they closed.

Elizabeth allowed herself to be led from the cemetery and sat in total silence on the flight back to London. She had declined to attend the family gathering at Les Cyprès, the Baathus château. Hunched in the back of the car during the drive to Lexington, she neither moved nor spoke.

When we arrived, she went straight to her rooms. Silently, fiercely, she motioned us to leave. And she stayed there. Hour after hour. Then day after day. In silence.

No speech, no sound of any kind was allowed. When we entered with food, or tried to speak to her about a doctor ... about help ... she looked at us as though our words were causing physical agony.

My parents grew more and more distraught at her muteness. I tried to calm them. I knew Elizabeth would recover. She would see it as her duty. To Stephen, her son, a duty of care. A duty not to cause further suffering to people who had been so full of love for her. Elizabeth even suffered selflessly.

After four days we heard a scream. Long and high. And then another and another. We raced towards her rooms. When we reached her, she was frantically trying to close the window.

"I have lost him. He's gone. Just now. He wanted to go. He wouldn't stay. I couldn't hold him. I had him in here." She hugged herself, shaking violently. "Come back, Hubert! Come back! Please, please, Hubert! Come back!" She turned to us, desperate. "I didn't want to wake him. He was so quiet. He was lying asleep, in me. I was afraid you would wake him. When you came to talk to me. Afraid that ... he would waken. And he would go. Oh, Hubert! Hubert! He has just left

48

me. He fought his way out of me. I am empty, Hubert. I am empty. I am empty."

We stood there. Petrified, made into stone by her pain. Unwilling, frightened witnesses to extremis.

Later she agreed to have the family doctor visit her. They remained together quietly talking for hours. When he emerged he told us she would sleep. Possibly for days, on and off. And she did.

It was finally over.

Twelve

"We've been approached by Derwent Harding PLC with an offer for Alpha Publishing. We're obliged to consider this offer."

"We shouldn't have gone public when we did," I said to my father. We were all at a hastily arranged family dinner.

"Yes. Well, Ruth, the Board was very keen at the time. And even though I'm chairman, as a family our contribution is minimal."

"You know, Father, I'd thought of trying to start a book publishing division at Alpha. Perhaps in a few years' time, when William is older."

"You've never mentioned this to me before."

"Perhaps I wanted to surprise you."

"That's something you have never found difficult. Ruth, we have our responsibilities to the company to consider."

"A kind of corporate noblesse oblige is it, Father?"

"In a way, yes. We're still the major shareholders," he continued. "But it's the Board's opinion that this is a serious offer and it must be taken to the other shareholders. I shall offer to resign as chairman."

"What will happen to Alpha if it accepts the offer?" I asked.

"Well, it will still trade under that name, but it will be owned by Derwent's. It does mean that our titles will have greater development opportunity. It's a very good idea really."

"Elizabeth?" He turned to her. Still in black. Nearly four years later.

"I feel that whatever the Board decides should be agreed by us. I've never made a contribution to Alpha."

"Your grandfather created the company. It wouldn't exist at all were it not for him," my mother interjected.

"Neither would we for that matter," I replied.

"Ruth." My father spoke. Almost sadly. "You know, my dear . . . though I'm pleased you had the idea of a publishing division, it wouldn't have sat well with the magazines. I'm certain the Board would have opposed it."

It was finally agreed that the chairman of Derwent's would come to Lexington for lunch the following Sunday. In order to meet the family. The **future** of Alpha could be discussed in congenial surroundings.

"It's all agreed then?" My father looked at each of us in turn. We nodded our consent.

I shivered suddenly. Perhaps the veil the angel wove had fluttered?

Thirteen

Wooden doors open from the main hall in Lexington into a large, high-ceilinged drawing room with an enormous French stone fireplace.

On either side of the fireplace two Aubusson-covered sofas face each other—in military precision as though standing guard over the low, almost black-green marble table. At each end of the room, two sets of wooden double doors can be glimpsed behind two exactly matching arrangements of tall-stemmed red roses standing on round tables covered in tapestry. A number of black high-backed chairs with studded arms defy anyone to sit on them.

Dark hangings on each side of the fireplace reflect, in their greenness, the distant view past the courtyard down to the park and the almost hidden lake. The walls between the French windows are bare except for the outer folds of heavy green velvet curtains. It is an austere, dark room.

A small sitting room-library opens off the north end of the main room. It is used for cards, chess and reading.

The dining room, with its long, dark mahogany table, silver candlesticks and one huge religious painting, is a room which could easily have been a chapel.

All the rooms are a study in darkness. Though the French windows imply a welcome, somehow the light stays politely away.

It was through these rooms that Sir Charles Harding followed my father into our lives.

He was a man in his late forties, of considerable height with a large, almost primitive face. He did not smile as I offered my hand to be most briefly held in his.

He turned towards Elizabeth. She was dressed, as always, in black. Did she understand how the contrast dramatised her paleness? That it gave her a power she did not have? No, such instincts were not Elizabeth's. They were mine. The unmade-up face and the severity of her hairstyle gave her the appearance of a nun. I saw the barest flicker of surprise as he looked at her.

My mother, who had been checking final arrangements for lunch, arrived. She received a bow from him and a polite acknowledgement of her outstretched hand.

Sir Charles Harding complimented her on the beauty of the roses. My mother glowed at this tribute to her secret passion.

Just as they seemed to delineate certain parameters of the room, the roses also seemed to structure my mother's week. Each Monday and Thursday they were ritualistically placed by her into their dark green porcelain prison. Parkdirektor Riggers—perpetual flowering—and as masculine in the tall erectness of their habit as they were in their name.

In a small room off the kitchen, canvas gloved, twice a week she picked, from her surgical array of instruments, secateurs that sharply cut to exact predetermined length each helpless victim, as it lay on its shiny chrome operating table. Then she took a small, sharp, dagger-like knife and neatly made a half-inch wound at the base of each green stem.

In her soft cashmere sweaters and her sensible skirts—sometimes still in her Panama hat—she should have presented to a loving daughter a vision of matronly serenity, engaged in that most soothing of activities, flower arranging.

Now, the ever perfect hostess, she led us all through to lunch.

"I can assure you all," said Sir Charles, seated on my mother's right, "that I've no intention of pursuing this bid if it's unacceptable to you." He paused. "It is not my way." His voice was strange—its intonation slightly clipped and abrupt.

"Of course, Sir Charles," said my father. "We appreciate you saying that. But we have considered the matter, we're content with the decision we made last week."

"Concerning the name?"

"Yes."

"As I said to your Board," Sir Charles continued, "that's not a problem. Nor will it ever be. We can make it a fundamental issue in the drawing up of the Heads of Agreement. I understand family attachments to business. *Buddenbrooks* is one of my favorite books."

"Ah. Yes. Mann," my father replied. The tone of his voice was ambiguous. It was not possible to establish what he thought of *Buddenbrooks*, or whether his attitude to it was influenced by some anti-German prejudice he'd never voiced before.

"I prefer *The Magic Mountain*," my father continued—although not with much enthusiasm.

"This conversation is tremendously literary, Sir Charles," I said. "But surely, however, your understanding of our proprietorial feelings for Alpha is based on the fact that your own family name has continued. And flourished. To the extent that you're now buying us out. Perhaps that's a more profound cause for understanding than even the most intimate reading of Thomas Mann."

"You are right."

The abruptness of the reply made his agreement almost a rejection. He turned towards Elizabeth. Sister Elizabeth. The tragic widow, infinitely more interesting than Ruth. By the very fact of her grief, and the way she bore it.

"Madame Baathus?"

"Elizabeth, please."

"Thank you. Elizabeth." His voice almost gave an extra *e* to her name.

And a strong lilt to the *Beth*. The name became music. Whereas mine was a short, sharp beat on the air.

Elizabeth spoke quietly. As always.

"I'm happy that the name will continue. Our grandparents would have wanted that. Father tells us the management believes that your company is the right one for them."

"A sort of marriage, perhaps?" I interjected. I wanted to break their . . . communion.

"Yes." Sir Charles was a man of few words.

"With a dominant partner of course." I pressed him.

"Of course."

"Is that your philosophy of business, and marriage?"

"It is, Mrs. Garton."

"Oh, Ruth, please."

"Thank you . . . Ruth."

Ruth. Quick beat. Harsh.

"We're discussing worldly matters, and in

worldly matters I like to dominate." Sir Charles smiled. Slightly.

"That's not a fashionable view," I replied.

"Indeed not. Marriage, however, is not only a worldly place. Women rule its real kingdom."

"Go on," my father said.

"It's my assessment that sometimes women misunderstand. They throw it all away. They're the centre of life. They hold its core. Yet they battle to be on the periphery of the world."

"And if, in time, they dominate the world?" I asked, smiling.

"Ah, well, they'll find it a very empty prize."

" 'Which of us has his desire? or, having it, is satisfied?' " I quoted.

He looked puzzled.

"It's Thackeray," I said.

"*Vanity Fair*, I assume?"

"Yes, Sir Charles." I was not certain who had won the point.

"A more cynical voice than Mann. Thackeray appeals to you more, I feel."

Damn. "And how does Lady Harding feel about her place in the world and life?"

"Lady Harding is dead."

Elizabeth turned slightly towards him. I watched their eyes meet. The banality of the power of pain was clear to me again.

"I'm so sorry," I said.

"Ruth couldn't possibly have known. I'm sure Sir Charles understands that."

Thank you, Elizabeth. Silently.

"Of course. There's no need to apologise."

"Sir Charles, you want us, as a family, to sell all our shares. Not just the proportion which would give you control."

My father was anxious, as always, to get back onto a less dangerous topic than men, women, life and death. The worldly world was a place he could manage.

The discussion continued—discreet, polite and very firm on Sir Charles's part.

Dominick arrived for tea. And to collect me. We had arranged to attend a concert with his parents, who were on a short visit to London.

"I must leave the arena then, Sir Charles." We shook hands.

"You've already made your position clear, Ruth. As I would guess you normally do."

I smiled briefly, and left. I had spoken of an arena other than that of business. Could he guess?

Hours later, Dominick lay on me. And whispered love again. And again. Perhaps the music in his own head made him deaf to my silence.

Fourteen

"Ruth." A downbeat. On the phone, a week later.

"I feel I may have been rather abrupt when we met last Sunday. Perhaps you and Dominick . . ." Wait for it, Ruth. "And your sister, Elizabeth, would care to have dinner with me next Thursday."

"You've asked Elizabeth?"

"No."

I waited. Always wisest. He was uncertain of himself. No doubt an unusual experience for him. He came, perhaps knowingly, into the trap.

"I felt it . . . inappropriate . . . after all she is . . ."

"A widow."

"Yes."

"A grieving widow."

"Indeed. Indeed. I could see that."

"You're not suggesting, Sir Charles, that I should ask Elizabeth on your behalf?"

"Of course not. Oh dear, I've embarrassed you. I'm so sorry. The entire undertaking was . . . ill-conceived."

"Undertaking! Hardly an undertaking, Sir Charles. Simply an invitation. I must speak to Dominick, but I see no reason why not."

"Oh, good." The relief in his voice was . . . noted by me. "Elizabeth I'll leave to you," I said.

"Absolutely," he replied.

"Till Thursday then."

"Till then."

Dominick, as always, was easy to persuade. Oh, kind face, brilliant mind. Oh, beautiful straw-coloured hair. Young man's body, why did you do this to yourself? Why didn't you send for your own lover? Why did you let me do these things to you? Where did you learn to betray yourself? Who taught you? Me. I suppose it was me.

We drove towards a small restaurant in May-fair—an unsurprising choice and therefore in its way a soothing one. I gazed at the creamy silky reflection of myself in the car's side mirror. I could safely assume that Elizabeth would be in black. I felt that Charles Harding's memory of his first dinner with Elizabeth should contain in its shadows my ivory-clothed figure. I thought how important it was to dress the part. Even when forced to wait in the wings.

Sir Charles was there before us. Elizabeth, by accident of course, was late. We sipped our drinks. And I felt him absorb my beauty with some interest, as we waited for the arrival of the one for whom the dinner really was intended. Grave, stark and with a graceful, understated apology, Elizabeth sat down.

Sir Charles had manoeuvred himself into our lives. I guessed that he rarely wasted time. And that the dinner would be the first of many.

I sat beside him. Elizabeth and Dominick sat opposite. Dominick, trapped, and Elizabeth less free than she knew. Elizabeth, believing herself to be part of a family outing, relaxed enough over dinner to entrance Charles Harding. I listened as she answered his delicately phrased enquiries.

"Yes, I've kept my studio. I go there to paint. Every day. Dominick once explained to me in mathematical terms the beauty of its proportions. But I love it for its light, all of which comes through the skylight. So I'm undistracted by windows onto gardens, or onto other houses. It's perhaps unkind of me to say so, but I find solitude even more important now."

"Why unkind?"

"Oh, because everyone—my parents, Dominick, Ruth in particular—has been so very supportive and good to me. And, of course, my darling son, Stephen, who has tried so hard to comfort me. It seems wrong . . . unfeeling . . . in the face of all this love to say that I need to be alone."

"And your paintings? What are you painting now?"

"Nothing."

"Nothing? But I thought you said you went there to paint."

"Yes. That's true. I go there to paint. But I do not."

I didn't know this. Will I ever know you, Elizabeth?

"Why not?" Sir Charles asked.

"I don't know. But I know it's right that I should go there every day. And one day it will be the right day."

Sir Charles cleared his throat. Touched, no doubt.

"So what do you do there?"

"I sit and wait."

"For inspiration?" I asked. This really had gone on long enough.

"I wait for the thing that is right for me to paint."

"Why not continue with the . . ." I remembered Hubert's phrase . . . "Enchantment?"

"Because that would imply that Hubert's death had not changed me."

We were all silent.

"I must stop now. I've spoken more about me than is . . ."

"Than is your wont."

"Yes."

"Well, here's to waiting . . . for what is right." Sir Charles raised his glass. I watched him drink her in. And I looked at Dominick, who innocently raised his glass to me and clearly didn't taste the pain.

Fifteen

"Tell me about Charles Harding." Helen and I were having lunch.

"Why?"

"Didn't you know he's trying to buy Alpha?"

"Does that matter to you? You've never expressed an interest in the company before."

"Let's just say I'm a hidden sort of person." I laughed.

"I don't really know him all that well."

"You know him better than I do. So give me some idea."

"Well, he's feared."

"By whom?"

"In publishing, of course. And in the City."

"Why?"

"He's very brilliant, intellectually. First from Oxford. And he's supposed to be a ruthless businessman."

"Is he?"

"No, not really. He's just successful beyond the laws of probability."

"God! Spare me the mathematical phrases."

"I'm not in Dominick's league."

"Helen, when I see you gazing out at me from the TV, analysing this or that company's results, I cannot help remembering the schoolgirl who traded her math prep for whatever perfume or lipstick she lusted after."

"Never yours, darling. You were always too pristine for such adolescent decorations."

"And anyway, Helen, I preferred to do my own prep."

"As now."

"What do you mean?"

"You're doing prep on Charles Harding."

"Well, as I said, he may be about to take us over."

"Hmmm."

Helen was as close to the concept of a friend as I ever had. Which was why I was particularly guarded around her. She had red, wavy hair and sharp, grey-green eyes. When she widened them during an interview, they made her most lethal questions sound benign. She had a certain female power much admired by women in my time. And used the gifts of nature to enhance a considerable intelligence—for the simple purpose of undermining powerful men. She was excellent at her job, fielded lust with some malice and succumbed, I guessed, with little pleasure. Our relationship had an element of mutual admiration and competition.

"Did you know his wife?"

"Felicity? Not really. I met her on just a few occasions, when she was being the token wife. Which she always did well, incidentally. She died four years ago."

"How did she die?"

"There was a long illness. A weak heart, I think. Though the end was very sudden."

"Children?"

"One. Grown up. I think he lives in America. It was a long marriage. There was never any scandal, that I heard of. Charles Harding is not one for the gossip columnists. Far too clever for that. Of course, there could be some secret. . . . But"—she paused—"on the surface it looks, my dear, as though what you see is what you get. Tycoon. Widowed. . . ."

I knew Helen well enough to have noted the pause and the equivocating words. . . .

"On the surface? What do you mean?"

She sat back in her chair and looked at me, a kind of question in her eyes.

She sighed. "Can I trust you, Ruth? This really is utterly confidential." I nodded. She paused and began to speak quietly.

"In the year before Felicity died—she had, remember, been ill for some time—he had a short affair with a young woman. She was . . . insanely

. . . in love. It was all extraordinarily intense, I gather. Very sexual, I would imagine. Anyway, he tried to end it. And she . . . killed herself. I knew her parents. It was all hushed up. Her father's a Queen's Counsel. Has enormous influence."

"And Charles Harding?"

"Well, he was—he was utterly devastated. Blamed himself entirely. Felicity died shortly afterwards. It was a double blow. To a man who I'd guess had felt himself capable of handling anything and anyone. I imagine he still feels very guilty."

Now I understood Elizabeth's attraction for him; she would be the perfect balm for a guilty soul. But what of the other side of Charles Harding? The "intensely sexual"? Was that for Elizabeth, too?

"Well, perhaps he'll meet a good woman." I smiled at Helen. I wanted to break the air of increasing intimacy between us. She took the bait. And became the public Helen.

"There aren't many of those about." She smiled back at me.

"Oh, yes there are. They're just as lethal."

We laughed our conversation to an end. And I left having learned a lot, but knowing that I had also revealed something of myself. Which, for me, was always too much.

Sixteen

Charles Harding had invited us all to his house in Gloucestershire for Sunday lunch. We would come bearing gifts. Or more precisely the gift of Elizabeth. He should beware.

Dominick and I drove in silence. Earlier, we had had another conversation about our marriage. He had lain beside me, physically satisfied, or finished—whichever—some lonely sensuality draining from his face. His blond hair fell limply across his forehead. His eyes, without his glasses, seemed somehow out of focus as he stroked my hair and whispered, "Ruth . . . you're breaking my heart."

I sighed.

"You've got what you wanted. Me."

We should not try to take what we know is not

Josephine Hart

ours. Even if by some miracle it becomes available to us.

"Do you know what a catastrophe is, Ruth?"

"I think so."

"No. In mathematics. Do you know what the word *catastrophe* means . . . in mathematics?"

"No."

"It means 'a system that disturbs another.' You have disturbed me. You've invaded me."

"Indeed. Well, there are other invasions."

I rose to shower. After the invasion. Modern woman, modern moves. So hygienic.

"We have too many of these conversations." My morning memory faded. We are now in the car.

"Maybe. You did pursue me, Dominick. And I'm not breaking any promises. Look. It's a beautiful day. Let's enjoy it. It will be interesting to see Sir Charles on home ground."

I was anxious not to have an obvious tension between Dominick and me. So unattractive, so demeaning. In front of Charles. So I placated him.

A woman adored—and of course I was—can do anything. Particularly when she makes so few mistakes. We were balanced. His love. My coldness. I wondered if Dominick understood how much he needed the agony. Probably not.

Charles Harding's house, Frimton Manor Farm, disconcerted me. Just outside a Cotswold village, it was a low-built, stone, seventeenth-century mansion. In place of the grandeur and opulence I had expected, the house exuded a mellowness and peace. It nestled behind a row of chestnut trees, which marked a sort of terrace at the end of a short poplar drive.

He stood in the stone porch to greet us. Then, he led us into a low-ceilinged drawing room in which a roaring fire, deep armchairs and an old carpet on the dark wooden floor all painted an image of the slow seduction of other times, and did so authentically. The house was not a lie. It was itself—in structure, decoration and odour. And if ghosts haunted it, I wondered if it was because they were at ease there. And perhaps found heaven a little bright.

The polite clichés began.

"How long have you lived here?" I asked.

"Since I was a boy."

"How lovely." Oh, God.

"When did your family acquire it?"

"My father bought it, when he married."

A pause.

He was polite but bored. I didn't blame him.

Another car arrived, and in a minute Elizabeth stood in the porch. I watched his face tense. He was no longer bored. I wished I didn't know these things. Elizabeth, in black again, shook hands briefly, then kissed me. Oh, those false sisterly kisses. False sister.

Within fifteen minutes or so, my parents had arrived. We ate a simple lunch, served by a couple

71

who seemed as much part of the house as the old silver and plain white linen napkins. Afterwards, we sat in a small sitting room for coffee. A portrait of a dark woman in a blue velvet dress gazed down at us. Surprisingly, it was Elizabeth who commented on its beauty.

"It's a portrait of my wife," he said.

A little silence.

"It's four years . . . now . . . since she died."

Murmurs of sympathy. Polite. Of no greater intensity or sincerity than an apology for disturbing someone who had been sleeping. "So sorry. Did I disturb you?" Nothing could disturb the subject of the portrait anymore. I wondered, had Felicity ever disturbed Sir Charles? Other than in death.

"Felicity loved this house. She loved country life. Rarely came to London."

"And you?"

"In those days I liked applause. When I was younger, London seemed a better place to find it than here."

"Well you have been much applauded." My father spoke.

"A little. In my own world."

"And internationally. Your work for . . ." Father mentioned an international charity for refugees.

More desultory talk of success, and its necessary companion—adherence to a good cause. Slowly, Sir Charles allowed a portrait—a most attractive portrait—to be painted of himself. For Elizabeth. Surrounded by her family.

And as he stalked her, I stalked him. I was not certain, watching him, which of us had more practice.

Did Elizabeth remind him of Felicity? There was no physical resemblance. Felicity's portrait was that of a petite, dark-haired woman in a blue dress. But other qualities perhaps? Spiritual qualities? Who can tell?

Memories—the living with them, and the killing of them—blur so much of daily life. We pick today's bouquet of feelings, sounds and smells, for tomorrow's contemplation. Tomorrow, Charles Harding would add today's miscellany to his gathered images of the past. And, perhaps, they would include me.

Seventeen

Where does all the time go to?

It goes to grow children and grey hairs. It goes to grow adolescent beauty and cancers. To grow the couple in their coming together and their separation. And at the end of all time we mark, it sweeps us up and away. An efficient hausfrau, a diligent harbinger of the next generation.

And time brought Charles Harding to Elizabeth and made them a couple.

It did so quickly, quietly, with utmost discretion. It moved so fast it disarmed me.

For the widow had been won. Back to life. She had been mesmerised by the intensity of Charles Harding's pursuit. And she was no doubt anxious, to live for others. Particularly her son, Stephen. A new pattern was established. With new players. Lexington absorbed Charles Harding for weekends and special anniversaries, as once it had absorbed Hubert.

William and Stephen, "the boys," became even closer. In their times together I could detect only love. And in their childish battles—they seemed to fight clean. But who can tell?

In small, careful ways I increased my influence on Stephen, Elizabeth's son. Particularly in the early years of her new marriage. At a time when Charles sought connection with his stepson, I forged a deeper bond with my . . . what? Nephew? No. False sister. False nephew.

Elizabeth was a quiet, gentle mother. Good, and kind. There was no question that Stephen adored his mother. But I was a more captivating companion. Subtly, I increased his adoration.

I was an intriguing aunt. I had a certain wildness, a sense of adventure that Elizabeth lacked.

Of all Elizabeth's possessions, Stephen was the most accessible to me. Our temperaments matched in some way. A wayward streak, perhaps.

It pleased me a lot when, at Lexington, he would call out, "Aunt Ruth, you're so funny," or, "Oh, come on, Aunt Ruth. Challenge me," or, "Test me on this, Aunt Ruth," or, "Let's go, Aunt Ruth. Let's go."

It pleased me, this application of my power. It

would have pleased me more had Elizabeth ever seemed distressed. But she remained serene.

Was such serenity a fault? Are you certain you approve?

Eighteen

Over time, I found I noted everything about Charles Harding. I had an appetite for facts about him. His body had a density about it, as though it had no hollows. As though it were a statue. His legs implied not speed but power. And when he stood before a window, he effectively blocked the sun.

When he spoke to others, I felt it clearly on my skin. Yet whenever he spoke to me, he came blurred down the line.

Sometimes, looking at him, I thought of the story Helen had told me. It was impossible to exploit, I was aware of that.

"There's nothing Elizabeth looks forward to more than your visits."

Charles and Elizabeth were welcoming us to Frimton Manor.

Dominick collected our things from the back of the car.

Elizabeth smiled, opening her arms to us. Stephen raced towards William and me.

Then, Elizabeth's kiss.

"Charles is right. I'm always full of happiness at the thought of your arrival."

Sometimes Elizabeth's happiness disgusted me. Literally. I felt disgust.

"But you see us regularly at Lexington at the weekends."

"Yes. Yes. But it's . . . just different here. It becomes a treat."

Charles was in fine, generous form. The mogul now spent only four days a week in his office. "Besotted," I had read in a magazine in a doctor's waiting room. "Besotted" by his new wife—"the artist, Elizabeth Ashbridge."

Elizabeth Ashbridge is not an artist, I had sighed at the journalist's idiocy. Elizabeth Ashridge is a reasonably competent painter of skies.

We sat down to eat—a group united by blood, by love, by hatred, a fairly common combination—and we drank to the success of Dominick, this man who had stayed much longer in my life than I had ever intended. He had just become the youngest ever head of Government Statistical Service at the Treasury.

"You must be so proud of him, Ruth."

"Ruth's pride is like so many things about her—understated," Dominick replied.

"Oh, but underneath she's glowing." Elizabeth raised her glass.

Charles addressed me. "Ruth. When William's older, do you still want to set up that book division you once mentioned?"

"Maybe. Why?" This is not how I want to speak to you. These are not the words.

"Ruth, you had so many ideas. The kind of books you wanted to publish. Charles is right. It would be . . ." Elizabeth speaks for me.

Who are you to know what is good for me? How dare you speak of my life? You two. As a couple. For my happiness.

"Ah, you're so encouraging. But Dominick is . . . uncertain. Darling?"

"Ruth would be brilliant at anything she did. There's no doubt about that. It's an interesting idea. But, let's wait—William is still young, and Ruth enjoys being with him a lot," Dominick replied, on my behalf.

"Well, Ruth, what would be the first book you would publish—a daring novel by a new young writer?" Charles asked.

"Absolutely not."

"Why?"

"There are enough books in the world already."

"You astonish me."

Josephine Hart

"I always at least try . . . to astonish you."

"But . . ." Dominick started to speak.

"Ruth, I think is teasing us."

Oh, sweet Elizabeth.

"No dear—I'm not. I'd like to re-issue some oddities—*The Laws of Sparta*, or *Diary of an Erotic Life*—in little pocket-book size. My first title would be *The Devil's Dictionary*."

Silence. Neither Elizabeth nor Charles smiled.

"I don't know the book."

Of course you don't, Elizabeth.

"Is it amusing?" Charles asked me.

"Yes."

My husband looked at me.

Charles said, "You have a very private mind, Ruth."

"What an extraordinary phrase, Charles. I always see myself as very open."

"You're not. If you decide to pursue your plan in the future, I'll help. But I'd need to establish whether you had a private passion which you'd bring to the public—or if not, whether you're an effective arbiter of public taste."

"Which do you think, Charles?"

"I would think not the latter."

"You know, Charles, you understand Ruth very well." I heard the note in Dominick's voice.

"Not better than you, Dominick."

"Private minds—anything that's hidden always fascinates us."

"Dominick's right." Elizabeth spoke.

And what would you know of hidden things, Elizabeth? You, who have lived with my hatred for years. Unknowing.

"Well, I've known Ruth longer than anyone. What she hides most often is her brilliance . . . because she . . ."

Dominick laughed. Or rather made a sudden, abrupt sound that used the mechanism we know as laughter. The rictus on the face . . . the force to expel the air through the lungs. All this effort to cover his pain. But then laughter is never passionate.

"Ah, I hear their car." Charles rose. My parents had been lunching with someone from my father's old regiment, who lived in the vicinity. They joined us for tea.

"Let's go into the garden and watch the boys."

We all became an audience. We watched their hardy, wiry little legs collide at speed, and yet not break. And our heads were filled with screams that would have turned our blood to ice, had we not seen the boys ride the screams to laughter.

Bodies, warm and dirty, threw themselves at us. We held them tight, and, as boys will, they struggled free again.

"I was in the Navy," Charles replied to a question from my father.

We were walking back towards the house. It was Armistice Day.

"Ah yes. The Senior Service." My father smiled at Charles. There was a silence. My father had been captured as a young pilot and had spent a year in Colditz. He never spoke of it. His elder brother had been killed over Berlin. His name was Michael. Whenever my father spoke the name, it seemed to me he quietly saluted a ghost.

"It's a mark of how old I have become." He sighed as we entered the house. "At last I can . . . occasionally and quietly . . . weep for the dead. For today, especially, we should acknowledge their sacrifice. It had a kind of glory."

I felt my father was summarising his view of the world almost as though he was preparing to leave it.

Later Dominick lay beside me—his long nakedness dense and heavy on the bed. Men do not look right covered in a sheet. Sheets are a woman's adornment. As the nakedness moved towards me I remembered the choreography. And afterwards. My cold eye. Questioning. I wondered if, in the cold eye, he found some peace.

Nineteen

Elizabeth considered it too cruel that I should receive by telephone the news of my father's sudden death from a heart attack. So she sent Charles to my home. At four in the morning. She knew William had accompanied Dominick to America, on a visit to his parents. She knew I was alone.

She gave me my chance. Her trust in me, and her kindness to me, gave me my chance. And it was my nature to take it. To bank down the sudden shock, to fight the pain. I would mourn later. Now, in this instant, I might know this man, Elizabeth's man—and through him know Elizabeth.

As Charles reached out to comfort me, I held the sympathy in his eyes and transmuted it into something else. It was my gift, you see. To find the centre. As he leaned towards me I moved—in such a way that his weight fell upon me as I collapsed with grief and desire against the wall.

When I opened my eyes, I saw in his face certain clues to my triumph. I saw that he knew himself. From past experience. That needs, past needs—buried now—propelled him towards me. He needed a sense of sin. To keep him in touch with his past.

I slowly opened the door to my dressing room. He followed me, down the steps. As I knew he would. Then, naked, arms above my head, I pulled on Elizabeth's silk slip—ageless enticement. And I thought I saw Elizabeth, ghost-like, stand beside me.

I lay on the floor, and he moved over me on all fours and grabbed my hair. As though to eat it. And then we separated and stood at either end of the narrow room. An image of my father flew across my sodden mind. And was lost. For I remembered that before I was even born it had been too late for us. The old anger crushed the pain that rose in me. And I acknowledged that it was now too late for everything.

My eyes beat Charles down and broke his resistance, as he walked, hypnotised, towards me again.

I took Elizabeth's pristine black shoe and licked the heel. I gave it to him. And quietly lay down. My eyes fixed on his face above me. Slowly he traced down the lines of my body with the gleaming heel of Elizabeth's shoe. Then he hesitated. I raised my back from the floor, for I saw the fear in his eyes. I wished to give him courage. Carefully, as though in a trance, he did what I wanted. And for the first time I wept for what I had become. Falling further away from myself, trailing Charles in his terror and delight towards the hidden face in the rock, which, unknowingly, he had begun to carve.

It was as I believed it would be. Elizabeth lay defeated beneath her black slip. Which I would not let him remove. A line long forgotten, came back to me. *Je est un autre.*

I bathed and dressed—in Ruth's clothes. We drove to the hospital in silence. I kissed my mother. She was as noble in grief as one would have expected. Elizabeth opened her arms to me, held me tight and consoled me. Perhaps an acknowledgement that he was my father, my real father. And not hers. Too delicate perhaps, to mention it.

Charles sat with my mother, held her hand and did not look at me. Finally, we all left for Lexington. Charles drove us. The widow, and two wives. One of them his.

An adult family mourning its patriarch is not stricken by grief so much as grieving. Even the sudden death of the old has about it the knowledge that it was foreshadowed.

As I stood in church my sadness was pierced by the light of an endlessly playing internal film of Charles and me. And of our bodies. I looked at Charles secretly, intensely. Hadn't Dominick once told me that gazing at certain objects alters their composition? Are you the same man, Charles? And I the same woman? Is there a persistent self? Somewhere?

I stood beside Dominick, who was exhausted after his night flight from America. And thought of the lie of the body and the mind.

At dinner my mother told us of her decision to stay on at Lexington. "This is where I spent my life with him. This is where I feel closest to him. Remember, John spent the week in London for many years, only coming home at weekends. I would love to see you all at weekends. Yes, that would be lovely. You know what joy the children bring me . . . brought us."

We knew her to be well cared for by Alice and Ben, who had been with us for years. With promises to carry on "coming home" for weekends, we left Lexington. Dominick went back to America for another week. He would return with William. We had considered a sudden trip back to bury "Grandpa" too traumatic for William, who had stayed with his grandparents. Elizabeth and Charles left for Frimton.

I waited in London. It was Charles's move next.

Twenty

Two days later his face appeared on the intercom screen. Distorted, almost disguised as himself, he seemed like a robot on a grey canvas. Then he stood framed in the doorway.

"I have a key, you know. For the main door. And for . . . Elizabeth's . . ."

"Studio?"

"Yes. Elizabeth is in Frimton. Ruth, I won't demean what happened between us with apologies or explanations. It's now a fact of both our lives."

I nodded.

"Ruth, I have thought a great deal about what I am going to say to you."

"Thank you."

"It was essential to think, Ruth. These are grave matters."

"And we have full knowledge. But perhaps no longer full consent."

"What?"

"Oh, it's a definition. Of sin."

"My wife ... my first wife, was a Catholic. I remember now. Grave matter. Full knowledge. And full consent."

"Exactly."

"But you're not Catholic, Ruth."

"No. But religion has always fascinated me."

"Oh."

"I surprise you?"

"In every way, my dear."

Ah ... "my dear."

"I assume you want some form of absolution."

"No. No, I want to tell you ..."

Tell me nothing, Charles. Tell me nothing. I am familiar with sin ...

"Let's see. I assume you've come to tell me that 'this will never happen again,' and to warn me."

"You insult us both."

I might win.

"We have a choice. This will sound very cold. Very calculating. Forgive me. Our choice is order or chaos."

"Well, define 'order' for me, Charles."

"The order of denial. Or the order of ... deceit."

"And chaos? What about chaos?"

"Chaos of discovery. And the destruction of our families."

"And?"

"And you, Ruth, as I have observed, are built for ordered deceit."

"And you?"

"I don't know. On the surface, perhaps. Even more than you. But I don't know."

"Elizabeth?" I ventured.

"The first rule, Ruth, is that you will never mention Elizabeth when we are together . . . like this."

"Rules?" The rules of engagement.

"Yes. You see, Ruth, we match each other."

"Perhaps."

Children alone in the dark who have never been happy or good.

Twenty-one

I, who believed myself a master in most things, now began my apprenticeship to Charles Harding.

I had believed him to be my victim. But he had been more willing than I knew. I had sought to trap. And was trapped, in a world of my own making. Which he came to dominate.

Nothing prepared me for my hungers, which, if not assuaged, would surely devour me.

Charles was not untouched by me—he had needs, too. But he could place limits on his desire. Whereas I had none. So I learned fear. But I never told my fear to Charles. Why arm one's master? He was already strong enough.

Charles was the stronger. And the stronger is always feared. "Better to be feared than loved"?

Best to be feared and loved. Can they exist together? They almost always do.

Why does the child love? Fear of abandonment, when sustenance is still needed. Is it the same with "love"? But that is not the correct word. What is the word—when one body feeds another? I had been worshipped by Dominick. I had seen his fear. Of abandonment.

Now it was my turn. It always comes around. Your turn, for pain, for knowledge. The knowledge you wish you had not attained. But it comes. For no one can do your knowing for you.

Elizabeth's studio moved into the pattern of my lusts. Once, just once, I led a trapped Charles past blank, upstanding canvasses, and the blind blue skies she had painted were mocked by me—by my actions. In silence, though with sighs. And Elizabeth's . . . things . . . moved deeper into the pattern of my needs.

Over years, the lie became a habit. We wore it well. My lifetime of small deceits had made me a skilled exponent of a dubious art.

Had Charles learned his capacity for treachery early? Or had it suddenly blossomed in that short, fatal relationship of long ago? In the year of Felicity's death.

Perhaps his was just a natural talent. I feared him too much to delve too deeply.

And I sometimes wondered, did he not fear another tragedy? Or were Elizabeth's innocence and goodness his great protection?

Our times together, easily arranged—we had "privileged information"—were compulsive, fierce and never satisfying. They became a spiral staircase into rooms the doors of which we should never have opened. And I led the way. My first obsession leading to the next.

Twenty-two

꿿

William Garton   Summer Term
Age: 12   Class: IA

Housemaster's Report
William is a grave child. In many ways almost old-fashioned. He is, however, well liked by the other boys, although, and we have spoken about this before, he has been the subject of some bullying in the past by two of the more rumbustious personalities in his year.

As you will see from the other masters' comments, William's academic work is very good—particularly in mathematics—not surprising when we consider his background! We look forward to watching him prosper further on his return to us in September.

Andrew Brown, Housemaster

William's serious approach to his work and his generally quiet demeanour has made his first year with us most successful.
Keep up the good work, William.

Broughton West, Headmaster

William does well at Latin. A very real achievement, when we consider that when he came to us his grounding in the subject was not all that it should have been.

Carl Donn, Latin

William has made steady progress in French. His prep is always meticulous. And on time! Well done, William. I gather the family intends spending some time in France this year. This may improve William's accent, which tends to be a little heavy.

Alistair Knight, French

William is top of the class in mathematics. I believe I can claim only a small responsibility in this matter. Nature vs. Nurture? No argument here, I feel.

Duncan Heychurch, Mathematics

SIN

★ ★ ★

William is making good progress in English. He works hard. His written work is exceedingly neat and tidy. What he lacks, I feel, is style. A little more reading perhaps? I have prepared a recommended list—which I attach—as holiday reading. Sorry, William!

James Sanders, English

William pays attention in class. He is progressing steadily, and his contribution to class project work is always interesting and constructive.

Michael Moore, Geography

William is good at history. His memory for dates and names is excellent. His essays, though factual and accurate, do not (as yet) show flair.

Brian Johnson, History

Alas, William is not an artist. He is always a pleasure to have in class and does his best. We persevere. However, I think even at this early stage we should consider dropping this subject after O levels.

Miles Masterson, Art

William is an excellent tennis player. He represented us brilliantly in our last tournament with Eton. His swimming is powerful, and his speed will improve greatly if he can find greater

rhythm in his breathing. He is not a gymnast—
but we can't be everything, can we? Congratu-
lations, on winning the school Under 16 tennis
championship.

Arthur Caldwell, Physical Education

William made a very impressive cabinet in his
design and technology project this term. He
seems to enjoy the subject.

Corin Morgan, Design and Technology

Overall, William's health has been excellent this
term. As you know, he suffers from a slight
stammer when excited. I'm confident he will
grow out of it. All in all, a healthy and quite
happy child.

Megan Owyston, SRN, Matron

Underneath were dates. For the beginning of the
next quarter. Future time. Structured. Organised.

Confidential
Dear Sir Charles and Lady Harding,

Stephen is gifted and charming. A seductive and
potentially dangerous combination. We have spoken of this before. I have seen these "blessings"
before. The incident in the tower, while not in
itself a cause for great worry, must not however
be ignored. It was, I feel, a warning to us all.

While Mr. Blake may believe that "the road of

excess leads to" etc., history does not prove Mr. Blake right. I do not suggest Stephen is a genius. He has however an outstanding intelligence. It is wise to remember Dryden's dictum "Great wits are sure to madness near alli'd, / and thin partitions do their bounds divide."

I feel that Stephen will develop the calm he needs so much in a smaller house, which we intend setting up next term for our "scholars." The house will be run by Mr. & Mrs. Trent. You will be interested to know that Mrs. Trent is, in a minor way, a landscape artist. They are a couple of great kindness and understanding.

You will see from the attached report that Stephen's performance is erratic. Exceptional in some subjects, undisciplined in others.

As it was impossible for you to attend my suggested meeting before the end of term, I was anxious to write to you to voice my opinion.

Since my own son's tragedy, I have become slightly more daring in warning parents of potential danger in the extraordinary experience of "bringing up" children.

Yours sincerely,

Broughton West.

Broughton West, Headmaster

I found this letter many years after it was written. Elizabeth took nothing, you see, when she left.

Memories. Voices, indistinct. But then memory is never pure. And recollection is always coloured by the life lived since.

Were they true, to their time, the adolescent voices that now seemed to flood the room? Was the undertone of anger in Stephen's defiant laughter true? As he stood there and denied allegations of recklessness and irresponsibility during Charles's investigation of "the incident in the tower"? And William's passionate defence of his hero—was the intensity of his innocent adoration still clear?

Perhaps, replaying old scenes we are seduced by ghost musicians. I turned towards them. As though a strand of my hair was caught in the instruments they seemed to play—tugged into old time. And I heard William's voice.

"Uncle Charles ... honestly, please try to imagine it. . . . Stephen, standing there on the parapet, high above us all. Gosh, he was brave, Uncle Charles. And, Hendricks—ghastly, bullying, mean Hendricks trapped in the quad and Stephen crying out:

" 'FRIENDS, BOLDONIANS, SCHOOL PREFECTS, LEND
    ME YOUR EARS;
  I COME TO SHAME HENDRICKS, NOT TO PRAISE HIM.
  THE PAIN THAT BULLIES CAUSE LIVES AFTER THEM.

THE COWARDICE IS OFT INTERRED IN THEIR RE-
PORTS;
SO LET IT *NOT* BE WITH HENDRICKS.' "

"And then, Uncle Charles, the head boy, Oldham, shouting: 'Harding! What the hell do you
think you're doing?'

" 'I am, Oldham, drawing your attention to injustice and bullying.'

"Oh, Uncle Charles, you would have been so
proud of Stephen. Please let me tell you the rest.
Please."

"All right, William. Carry on, carry on."

Charles sighed as he nodded ruefully to William, who in a fever of excitement continued his
tale, playing the parts as he went along. Stephen,
moving from foot to foot, embarrassed, but shyly
pleased with this hymn to his daring.

" 'You're a bloody junior, Harding. . . . You're
not here to draw my attention to anything.'

" 'What, Oldham? Are you not an honourable
man?'

" 'Get down, Harding, get down this minute.'

" 'Have prefects lost their reason? Bear with me,
Oldham. . . .'

"And then, Uncle Charles, with all the boys
stamping and cheering, Stephen bowed to us all,
and got down from the parapet."

And the voice of the storyteller faded. And suddenly died. I sat quietly for a minute. Then I picked

up Stephen's summer term report. He was four-
teen at the time.

Summer Term   Stephen Harding
Age: 14   Class: 3A

Stephen is, in a word, a scholar. He has been
first in class since he arrived here. I have had no
problems with his work—in either accuracy or
presentation. I believe from conversations in the
common room that this is not a universal experience with Stephen. However, his cleverness
is not resented by the other boys. That statement alone summarises much of Stephen and his
charm. I look forward to teaching him in the
future.

Carl Donn, Latin

Stephen has a natural flair for Greek. He has the
heart of a classicist combined with the temperament of an artist. We await development!

Xavier James, Greek

Stephen is an outstanding pupil, particularly in
French literature. He is currently entranced by
Baudelaire, though I feel I ought to inform you
that he has moved well past the class curriculum
in respect of this author. Stephen's sardonic use
of the quotation "calme, luxe et volupté" for a
class essay on "House Atmosphere" rather gave

the game away! I have specifically forbidden "Les Fleurs du Mal," a decision with which I feel confident you will be in full agreement. Let us hope this does not dampen Stephen's enthusiasm for French.

Alistair Knight, French

Stephen's essays are in reality "short stories." They demonstrate a maturity that is extraordinary. His rather wild sense of humour takes the sting out of some of his more morbid writings.

James Sanders, English

No mathematician he. What more can I say? We do our best to inculcate, against his natural inclinations, the rudiments of mathematical principles, and mostly fail. I suggest after 0 levels that the subject be dropped entirely. No one benefits. Stephen is however always pleasant in his behaviour and ironically I always enjoy having him in the class.

Duncan Heychurch, Mathematics

It is not wise in my opinion that Stephen has allowed himself to become so enamoured of some subjects, that others seem to bore him. Geography is important. I gained Stephen's attention only once—during the debate "Geography Is History." His subsequent essay on the subject was brilliant. I have, in fact, taken the liberty of submitting it for the "Ovington Award" this year. It would be a great honour for the school were he to win, though not necessarily "character building" for Stephen. A familiar dilemma.

Michael Moore, Geography

Stephen enjoys history and is always in the top three. His essays are as memorable for their style as for their content—a rarity amongst historians! He is a pleasure to have in the classroom and he contributes much to debates.

Alex Dunnington, History

Though reasonable at science, Stephen's behaviour in the lab this term was, on one or two occasions, potentially dangerous. A calmer, more considered approach is called for. Perhaps his move to Mr. Trent's house will achieve what is necessary in this department.

Colin Thornton, Science

Stephen is above average at art. He is not however as committed as one would have expected. Nevertheless, his exciting use of colour and his interesting view of even the most basic object is always fascinating. Could surprise us all—in art, that is.

Miles Masterson, Art

Stephen's work in the gymnasium is reasonably good. His tennis is adequate—he seems not to make much effort—perhaps intimidated by his cousin William's success. Stephen's tendency to asthma makes swimming "not his favourite sport." We persevere in this element. Not a natural one for Stephen, I'm afraid.

Arthur Caldwell, Physical Education

Stephen had two minor attacks of asthma this term. We are increasingly aware of the psychosomatic element in asthma. The more Stephen "calms down," the better it will be for him. The move to the Trents' house is welcomed by me. I have long recommended this idea.

Megan Owyston, SRN, Matron

I put these reports, which I now know almost by heart, back in their carved wooden box. And picked up a crumpled article from years ago called

The Artist in His Time
Brannington Orchard, Art Critic

Is it a failure in the artist to be unfashionable? Each artist lives in his or her own "modern" time. Are we simply looking for landmarks? Ever hoping, through a recognisable historical pattern, to tame something essentially timeless. The artistic impulse.

I post these questions—perhaps awkwardly—because Miss Elizabeth Ashbridge is that most awkward thing, an unfashionable artist. Her work has been exhibited occasionally over the past ten years. It is rarely reviewed. Perhaps an understandable decision on the part of editors who have more "fashionable" artists to cover. Nevertheless I contend that though not contemporary—in the normal usage of the word—and though not an innovative force (the very nature of genius is ever to innovate), Miss Ashbridge is an artist worthy of our most serious appreciation.

Skies, mostly English—her obsession—are executed with a growing note of desolation. As though the tension between the narrowness of our lives and the broad freedom of the skies was becoming clearer and ever more painful to her. Compare her earlier, charming "Blues London" with her more stark "Flight." A single slightly ragged cloud seemingly beating against the edges of the canvas, as though desperate for escape from a harsh, high, almost searing blue. One can see why it is naive in the extreme to dismiss Miss Ashbridge's work as that of a minor "lady" painter who has "a thing" about skies.

Her "Athens Revisited" is a major development from the work "Athens Morning." The latter, I believe, was executed on Miss Ash-

bridge's honeymoon when she was married to
Hubert Baathus. He was tragically killed early
on in their marriage. I also recommend "Studio
Sky." It has a haunting quality, as though the
artist was trapped in her studio, and, like Oscar
Wilde, trying to catch "that little tent of blue
which prisoners call the sky."

There are many other fine pieces, sympathet-
ically mounted in Adrian Carendon's small gallery in Mount Street. I recommend a visit.

Reports from strangers. Reports from a distant
land. The past.

Twenty-three

"I know."

"Know what, Dominick?"

"Ruth. I know."

Silence.

"I know." Again. And again silence. Silence gives consent. To the knowledge I would have kept from him.

Know. It has a heavy beat. Should I say, "I'm sorry"? Lie again? I take the coward's way. I say nothing.

"Ruth?"

I put down my drink. We were having dinner.

"Yes."

"Did you hear me?"

"Oh, yes."

"Don't you want to know how?"

"No."

I only want to know if you know who.

"I have only one question."

"Only one?"

"Yes. Will you continue?"

Silence. Oh, what a coward soul is mine.

"I see, Ruth, that once again you have risen to the occasion."

Does that sardonic note mean that I may be "let off"? Is that the phrase? So cheaply. I've won. I can be carefree. I am loved. And I love. Is it my fault that I do not love where I am loved? That I accepted the gift I should have rejected? But then he would have been unhappy. Perhaps not. If I had acted honourably from the start. Such harsh demands, Ruth. Such terrible penalties, Ruth. Listen. Listen to the man.

"I am rooted in you. From the day I saw you, I loved you."

Did love enter through the eye? I thought that was lust.

"You were a kind of perfection."

Like a formula. I had, perhaps, pleasing proportions. I wore the numbers 36 24 36. Draw it. Add some clothes, or not, as you like. Top it with a face. A vision of planes and pools. Dark brown, actually, for the pupils, black for the brow. Skin unpitted, the colour of full cream. And lips "bite red." The way they like it. And lower down, legs in proportion. Fine and long. Was that the geometry of his downfall?

So why does Charles resist? But he doesn't. Yes, he does. There's no not knowing that knowledge. I am the other. The addition. To Elizabeth. Again. Was he evenhanded, do you think?

As Dominick spoke, I tried to listen. I knew it was important. I tried. One should. He was in pain. The pain of isolation. The isolation of pain. I listened to his pain. It's hard to hear. One listens so rarely. Certainly can't feel it. Another's pain. Why does everyone in pain want to share it? There is no diminution. Me divided into your pain will not diminish it. Surely you knew that, Dominick? Your pain divided by my decent—yes, decent— concern, would not diminish it. And eventually, Dominick, I would grow bored by your pain. And wish to be the victim—just for a change. And now, listening to pain, I wanted to race towards pleasure. Any kind of pleasure. For relief.

"You had a kind of light around you. An intelligence. A quickness."

Speed of light? Do you know what you say, Dominick? How you pick your words from your version of the world.

"I see you, turning . . . on a point. Almost . . . towards me."

A pedestal perhaps?

"In my visions of you . . . you're always turning towards me."

Isn't that ironic? Listen!

"And this vision of you, as I reached towards it, kept turning towards me. Because I wanted it so much. It didn't move away."

Will he remember me as a vision? Like the man who fell in love with the face of a passenger on a ship, sailing away? Just a face. And stayed faithful. I might have been just a remembered face. And done no harm. Such an innocent thing. A face, when loved. From a distance.

"I thought . . . Ruth. It's her. It's Ruth. And so it always has been. Such a simple thing."

I should have let you go, Dominick. I should have known I was dealing with an idealist. An idealist in love. Worse than a romantic. Oh, infinitely. An idealist. Always faithful. Loyal. Trustworthy. Rare, of course, but not treasured. Few buyers.

"And now I don't know what to do. It's just impossible. . . ."

Yes, Professor. You have a dilemma. Indeed you have. What to do . . . with the pain. With the love. Too much love.

Should this be presented in percentages? Quantities? Liquid, perhaps? Comparatively? Statistically? Geometrically? In algebraic terms? If $x = ?$ I don't know. I'm not the mathematician. Just picked up some phrases. Extra love marks the critical point. What does one do with extra love? Add an extra ingredient? Bitterness? Some contrast? Hate perhaps?

"You have destroyed our past, it just seems to lead to now."

His past had been unpredictable. And the future . . . ?

Has a shadow. It falls across the path. We will stumble if we continue on the road.

"It's not, Ruth, that I could ever stop loving you. Ever. It is simply that I'm not brave enough to see you all the time and know what I know."

"No."

"I'm a coward."

"No."

"I'm afraid of you—in the morning . . . it's . . ."

Even I do not know the word. He continues: "And I fear . . . other . . . things."

Naked power. At night. But sometimes in the morning. Naked mornings. Morning power.

"Even the hidden sweetness in you when you touch or talk to William. I suppose I fear . . . my fear."

"So?"

"I'll just go."

Go? To where? And to what?

"I'll live apart from you. I can't . . . I can't live with you."

Oh, God. This is going to be very difficult. What will Charles say? Think, Ruth. Think. I could lose him. Charles.

Dominick is still talking.

"Elizabeth is giving up her studio here."

110

"Elizabeth." What is her name doing here? In this room. In this conversation?

"What?"

"I see I've got your attention. Charles means to spend less time in London. He's building her a special studio at Frimton."

"How do you know?"

"Because I talked to Charles."

"When?"

"A few days ago. I suppose he thought it more appropriate to tell me about the studio."

More appropriate? To talk to Dominick? About new "arrangements"?

"Did you talk on the telephone?" Freud always hated the telephone.

"Is that relevant?"

"No."

I just want to know how I was betrayed. For it is a betrayal. Within my world—with him—I thought I was hermetically sealed. No possible intruder. Even casual visitors. Not allowed. But now I feel the terror of the periphery. I feel the force that could trap me there forever. And an even stronger force that might propel me into an eternal free-fall. But I won't let this happen. I have hooks to hold on to. And though suspended above it, I am not in the abyss. Yet.

"I've lost you totally."

"What?"

111

These are unlucky words. I do not want to hear them. In case I learn to say them.

"Ruth, please. Please listen."

"Yes. . . . Yes."

"By moving into Elizabeth's studio I can see William in a familiar environment. It will be less traumatic for him."

"Yes."

"Is that all you can say?"

Collect your thoughts, Ruth.

"No. No, it's not. I think your decision is . . . is false. It's a false move. Don't make it."

"You astound me, Ruth. You're . . . an aberration . . . in some way."

"I thought you swore eternal allegiance to me."

"I don't remember that phrase."

"You're right, Dominick. I think you said you'd love me always. Something like that."

Well, Ruth. Make a decision. Quickly. Which is best? Make Dominick stay? Or make him go? Which is best? For your relationship with Charles. For your . . . suddenly . . . weakening relationship with Charles. Which is best?

Keep Dominick. Much better. A base. One must have a base for a secret life. Too obvious the other way. The unmarried woman with her married lover. No. Keep Dominick. He wants to stay. Such childish nonsense about the studio. It makes no sense. The pathetic business about William. William is at boarding school. And holidays and half terms are spent at Lexington. Stupid Dominick. Stupid? Dominick? Not words I'd normally put together.

So make him stay. Be subtle. Be slow. Just move. The way you can . . . towards the drinks cabinet. Now turn. Look a little sad. But slow sad. Let everything drain from your face so that, as you know, only sensuous silkiness remains. Watch his face. There is a tiny flicker. Hold on to it. With your eyes. Just hold it. But carefully, Ruth. Carefully. Say nothing. Silence. It is essential for concentration. For the concentration of your power. To achieve your will.

Now. Give him a drink. Stand close. Don't move. He must reach out for you. Otherwise it's impossible for him. For the future. Breathe deeply so your breasts move to a rhythm you know. Leave him now. You can feel the tension in him. Move to the sofa. Lie lengthways. Sigh. Sadly. And let one leg fall down so that the skirt of your dress falls away. A little. And just gaze. He is coming towards the sofa. Hold his eyes. Hold them. Sadly. And he is here. Above me. Now he is about to . . . and his hands betray him. Desperate. They search again for the way in. And it's over. I've won. I lie back. Dominick won't leave. Not this time. Not ever?

Twenty-four

"I'm sorry. I meant to tell you."

Charles and I. Time together. Regularly, in my home. So easy, when you are trusted. And when you know all the arrangements of the "others." Where they are. When they will return.

"About what?"

"My conversation with Dominick. About the studio."

"Oh, it doesn't matter. Elizabeth and I spoke of it this morning. I gather you're building her a studio in the grounds at Frimton. And that you will spend less time in London." My tone was cold.

"Yes."

Silence.

"If I can."

"Do you think you can?"

"I intend to try," he said firmly.

"Why?"

"I have surprised, in myself, a desire—"

"Indeed."

"A desire to do what is right. However hard."

"A passion for what is difficult."

"Perhaps."

I won't accept this. Don't say that. Stay calm.

"Charles, you're my only chance of . . . goodness."

"Ruth!"

"Yes. I've never betrayed you."

"To Elizabeth?"

"No."

"You would never do that."

An order. Obey it.

"Of course not."

Watch carefully. Search for . . . a degree of weakness. In his resolution.

"Charles. Within our world I have tried . . . I think I have been . . . true."

True to what? To what we've done. True to you. True to the things you hide.

He looked away. I knew his secret soul. It hid in his body. What would he do when he must kill it? Could he? He is dangerous, to me. He is strong. He may kill it. A death for me. A gift to Elizabeth. Another. Why not? No, I will triumph, in this. I must. Consider tears. No, liquid lies. He'd lacerate me.

He turned back to me.

"Dominick. Has he decided against the studio?"

"Yes. We were going to use it as a study for me. But it's unnecessary. I can easily work at home."

Try for normality, Ruth. Delay him.

"Work? At what?"

"I'm going to prepare an anthology . . . *Rejections*."

"What do you mean?"

"Oh, I'll research rejections great authors have suffered. An interesting idea, don't you think?"

"Good title."

"Yes. Excellent."

He smiles a little. Good. Good, Ruth.

"And Dominick?"

"Dominick is . . . content."

"I think he knows."

"Knows? No, Charles."

"But something in the way he looks at me."

No. No knowledge. Of you, Charles.

He is relaxing. He knows it. He wants to say fatal words. Stop him. He must steel himself. To mean them. Stop him.

"I have . . . a rage, Charles."

"A rage?"

"I rage for you."

And the fire jumped suddenly between us. He was engulfed. I fanned the fire with hair and

116

breasts and thighs. And then rolled him, shuddering, into quiet darkness.

And when it was over, there was anger. His awful anger. A different rage. Internal. Against himself. Then against me. I saw it in his eyes. In the bitter mouth. He moved, older looking somehow, towards the door.

He started to speak. But did not turn round.

"There is only one way, Ruth. I won't ever be alone with you again. Ever. If the chance occurs, I will walk out immediately. I must. You are . . ."

He passed his hand across his mouth. To stop the words.

"An occasion of sin?"

The hand fell away. Became a fist.

"I will do this, Ruth. I will do this."

Damn you! Damn you, Charles! Don't say anything, Ruth.

You're going to try. Aren't you? I can see that now. But I won't help you. Not at all. I won't help you. I will try to undermine you in every way. And remember. I am here. Waiting. Watching. Always ready.

He leaned against the door. He was so large . . . he covered it. As he so abundantly covered me. Oh, God. Then he was gone.

Silently, I screamed around the room. Dominick's room. I brushed against the globe. Spherical, completed, stomach-like thing . . . and beat my own stomach. Onto the warm honey of my skin came a darker mark—a blueness. Cold colour. I started to shiver. To feel the cold. I wound a woolen shawl of red around me. Blood-coloured. To warm me. I paced for hours round my prison. Then I remembered some pact that still existed, with a reality I had created. And, I feared, had to maintain.

I went to the bathroom to prepare for my husband's return.

That night and the next morning I gave no sign.

Appearance—a small clue to reality—is easily assembled by women, for deception. Though in England one must do this carefully. For it is more acceptable in England to feed the body than to clothe it. Though neither is deemed to be of importance. Yet we, like everyone else, can read the signals—the cardigan is as potent a garment as the blue waistcoat Goethe gave to Werther. A fatal gift.

Standing, hours later, as I waited for Dominick, I was simply and perfectly dressed. I wore a navy, belted dress. My pearls. Navy leather pumps. My hair was brushed to its normal gleaming condition. My face, after the application of soothing creams and the careful painting of a subtle mask, presented to my husband's eyes—the appearance of his beautiful wife.

That I had raged animal-like around my room. That I had been most deeply wounded. That thoughts of violence and ferocity had burst through all normal controls. That my life had arched back in agony, and snapped. All this was hidden.

For I was proud. I had been rejected. I was not to be rejected. Ever. Not in these matters.

The knowledge of the constant betrayal of Elizabeth had not been unpleasing. Waiting with that knowledge, that I might or might not impart. Whispering it. Silently. Through weekends and dinners. Only to myself. That had been a satisfaction of considerable depth. Now I was to lose that also. Unknowing, she had defeated me. Elizabeth. Stealing what was mine. For he was most assuredly mine.

I knew his agony. Could he bear it? For a while, perhaps. Would the habit of abstinence grow? Or would desperation mount? So that he would beg. As I begged him. Silently. Surely he must feel something, beating at the ramparts of his body.

Would I beg? No. For that would lessen his need. I knew him. It was essential in such an undertaking to know the enemy. He held from me that which was mine. Therefore he was my enemy. I would not show weakness to my enemy. Never. Pride. Strength. Patience. The seeds had been sown in him, and grew in me. He would come to gather his harvest.

Twenty-five

For one month, thirty days, Charles Harding deprived me of the very sight of him. Things—I had no words for them—seemed to flutter and die in me. Endless daily deaths in some small cavity within me. Somewhere to the left. I think the pain first emanated from there.

A weekend in Lexington was cancelled. On a Friday morning. Pressure of work. Elizabeth's voice. The sincerity of her apologies echoed round empty halls in my mind. And in Lexington. We were not invited to Frimton Manor.

I needed a plan. I had to see him. Could I trick him into seeing me? I used the nearest available and most potent weapon. My family. Particularly my son.

I rang Elizabeth. The right words tripped fluently from my lips. Phrases like "family gatherings." "The boys." "So close." "All together." And finally, "Mother's loneliness." Elizabeth agreed enthusiastically to a family half term at Lexington. I heard her win Charles's agreement.

Or do you secretly want to come, Charles? To Lexington? To see me? His distant voice—trapped by the phone as he answered her questions—beat a tattoo of desire on my skin. Yet I held on to the bars of myself and did not fail.

Half term at Lexington. Autumn days. The leaf-strewn lake a broth of winter colour. Browns, gold, ruby reds. And the sky—a high, cold, singing silver-blue. Ferocity had etched something high, cold and silver onto my face.

Charles was an animal at bay. One who knew he had walked into the trap. Because he had to. Because he wanted to? As we all gathered in the main sitting room, I decided to be merciless.

Damn you, Charles. To have thought of escape. Damn you. I would prefer you dead than not mine. His large body made sudden movements—startling—out of character, when he saw me. I walked deliberately towards him at the drinks cabinet.

"Are you in hell, Charles?" I whispered the words. "I hope you are."

"Hope he's what?"

"Happy at spending more time in Frimton."

"I always like to spend more time with Elizabeth."

Vengeance.

"And I with you, Charles. And I with you," said Elizabeth.

"A happy couple."

Do they get the note of irony in your voice, Dominick?

"Just like us." I smiled at him.

"Aha!" He responded.

"Dominick. You've definitely decided against the studio?"

"Yes. We really don't need it."

"I'm pleased. I don't think I want to sell it. I've been so happy there. It's been a lovely haven."

I remembered an intricate ballet of lust. Limbs and bodies angled so as not to harm the paintings. In her haven. Her husband and I. Shall I shatter her now? Take the hammer? But I will lose him forever.

"You had a marvellous piece in *The Daily* . . . by Brannington Orchard. Terrific for you, I would have thought."

"Thank you, Dominick. I can't connect to anything anyone writes about my painting. Even those who are kind to me. It's just something I have to do. Increasingly."

The compulsion of the artist. Even the most minor artists feel driven to develop their minor talent, often accompanying its development with major displays of temperament.

"Have to, Elizabeth? The only God, Art? 'Te Absolvo' always on His lips?"

Such was the bitterness in my soul. My soul? I had fed it such a diet over the years that it had long ago hidden, small and hungry, from my bitter offerings.

"I don't think you really mean that, Ruth," Elizabeth replied. "I know this is old-fashioned, but I believe that art should serve good."

"Dominick. You should work out a formula for good. If x equals kindness and y . . . equals . . . Let's see. There really aren't that many words that instinctively describe goodness . . . are there, Charles?"

I turned towards him, smiling. He looked back. Unseeing.

"Courage?" Stephen volunteered.

"Admirable, Stephen." He turned with relief to his stepson.

"But evil men have often been very courageous."

"Justice?"

"Aha. The pagan virtues seem to appeal to you." Listen to me, Charles.

"Pagan virtues, Aunt Ruth?" Stephen looked at me. Fascinated.

"Yes. The virtues before Christ. Hard virtues.

Masculine virtues." I spoke severely. The words demanded it.

"Well, Mum." William interrupted. "Which do Stephen and I have—the pagan or the Christian virtues?" I love the way William speaks. So gently. Dominick again. Dominick dominates.

Stephen turned to Elizabeth.

"You're both good boys."

"Aagh. Aaaaaagh. Oh, God, Mum. Never even whisper that in public." Stephen fell around the room, as though wounded.

"Sorry. Sorry, Stephen. Sorry, William." Elizabeth laughed.

"You did badly there, Elizabeth." Dominick smiled at her.

"I know, Dominick. I know."

"Perhaps Christ was fed up with all that macho stuff, and that's why he started preaching about meekness and about patience et cetera. And love with a capital L. Was he the first 'new man' do you think, Mum?"

"Stephen, this is quite sacrilegious." Said with a gentle smile. All her smiles were gentle.

"One can never show all the virtues at the same time."

Charles, as he spoke, concentrated his gaze on the boys. "The pagan and the Christian are virtues almost in opposition. Gentle courage? Meek justice? Fate decides what virtue your life depends on. For example, Stephen, you might discover that

124

only courage could save your soul. That you were kind, generous and loving ... but the Christian virtues were not required. Courage was the necessary virtue."

Look at me, Charles. Charles. Look at me. Like that, if you want. But I've got courage. Why haven't you?

"What is the greatest virtue, Elizabeth?" Dominick turned towards her.

Speak to me of virtue, Elizabeth.

"Oh, dear I find these things difficult."

"Go on, Mum." Stephen interjected.

"There's no single quality that cancels out the others. As Charles said, you can be cruel and courageous, or truthful and proud. I'm sorry, I'm not good at absolute statements."

Oh, come on, Elizabeth. Stop looking for sympathy. You're doing OK.

"The boys would like to hear ... it's important." I turned, bright-eyed, towards her.

"It's an attitude to the world. To others in the world. And to yourself. It's an attitude of ... It's a belief based on a personal commitment to do the right thing in all the circumstances of your life. And I suppose this is my philosophy of life: You must prepare for action ... by thought. Because evil action springs from evil thought. So you have to develop in yourself 'goodness of thought.'

"Good action will spring from that. I ... It
125

doesn't matter that . . . it doesn't always work. It's almost always hard."

Charles walked towards her. "Indeed it is, Elizabeth." He sat on the edge of her chair.

"So, it's in the soul . . . or heart, or mind?" I asked. With some interest.

Show respect, Ruth. The woman is sincere, Ruth.

"Yes." She nodded. "And it requires . . . everything."

His eyes are on her as on a god . . . goddess. This. This, perhaps I cannot fight. But fight I will.

"Mum. You're an angel. I always knew it." Stephen exploded from his chair. "But when you talk of being good, I just want to be bad. Let's race around the lake! William? Aunt Ruth? Come on, let me show you how fast I am." He held his hand out to me.

"I'll come later," William said. "I'm going up to the sheds—to fix my bike."

William liked to be alone sometimes. My independent, grave child.

"Will you come for a walk with me, Aunt Ruth?" Stephen asked.

I hesitated. I could not say, "I want to stay with Charles. Your stepfather. To see if I can destroy his will. His desire to leave me."

"Yes. All right, Stephen. You go on, I'll catch you."

"Great. See you later, Aunt Ruth."

They both jumped up like arrows speeding towards their target. The whoosh of their exit seemed to force the French windows open. They were gone. Youth had left the room. We sat silent for a moment and looked at one another. The way adults do. Indulgent.

My mother began: "I wonder, Charles. Would you drive me to Barnham? Could you bear it? It's only ten minutes' drive. I promised Claude that I would take her some of our tomatoes for lunch. Ben picked them this morning. I'd rather like to give them to her myself."

"I'm at your service, Aileen. With pleasure."

"Oh, I haven't seen Claude for ages, I'll come too," I offered.

There would be time surely, in the presence of two old women, both a little deaf and slow . . . for words. Maybe.

"But, Ruth. You never liked Claude."

Mothers! The things they know. The things they remember. A life before one's own memory. No wonder we long for escape. They'd devour us if they could.

"Nonsense, Mother."

"Do you pass through the village?" Dominick asked.

"Dominick, how many years have you been coming to Lexington? You have the worst sense of direction of anyone I know."

"Well, thank you, Ruth. But when we're here,
127

we don't leave Lexington all that much. Since I've never been to Claude's, how on earth would I know where it is?"

Marital banter. That's all, Charles. Don't look so worried.

"Well, let's start your education today. Come with us. Claude is a fascinating woman. She was in intelligence during the Second War." Charles. The peacemaker.

"Add to her war efforts, three husbands—all dead, conveniently—and considerable run of lovers."

"Ruth, darling, 'conveniently dead' is not how I would describe three men I knew and liked."

"Joke, Mother. Joke."

This is not as I had planned.

"To be honest, apart from the fascination of Claude, I want to get some petrol for the car. Let me drive the three of you there." Dominick rises.

"But, Charles, if Dominick is going it's hardly necessary for you to go as well." I tried. For time.

"Ruth. I'd love to see Claude. And I can direct Dominick."

He had escaped me.

They left. Elizabeth headed towards the kitchen to talk to Alice about lunch. I walked after Stephen to the lake.

"Hello, Aunt Ruth." A short silence.

"Do you know I'm reading *Madame Bovary* at school." He sought to impress me.

"And what do you think of her?" I asked him.

"Well, I think she was trapped ... you know ... within herself. No one set her free."

"That's very good, Stephen." He blushed at me. I played, a little, with the look in his eyes.

"I sometimes feel trapped ... by my asthma." Then, manly again, not wishing to seem as though he had looked for pity: "Do you know what Flaubert said when he was dying, Aunt Ruth?"

I did. Best to let him tell me.

"What did he say, Stephen?"

"He said: 'I'm dying and that bitch Bovary will live forever.'" He laughed. Thrilled with himself.

"Sorry about the word 'bitch,' Aunt Ruth. Learned it from my French teacher." More laughter. Whoops of laughter. Stephen had a wonderful laugh.

He took my arm.

"I think you're amazing, Aunt Ruth." He paused. Looked at the ground. "You're really ... really pretty. Aagh. That sounded ... yuck. Sorry. Sorry, Aunt Ruth." Suddenly, leaping in front of me.

"I'm going to swim across the lake, Aunt Ruth. For you. Show you ... how brave I can be. For you."

"Don't be ridiculous, Stephen. Go on up to the sheds. Help William with his bike." He looked at me. A question in his eyes. Then he shrugged.

129

Kicked a few stones and said, "OK, Aunt Ruth, OK."

Bored, I turned away. And started to walk home. Lost in my contemplation of Charles. How to get him back.

When I got to the house, Elizabeth was rolling the lemons to soften them. I chopped and scattered black olives onto the creamy pink and beige of the crabmeat. I chilled the wine and warmed the bread.

I went to my room to prepare myself. Before my lunch. With Charles. Then I rejoined Elizabeth and Alice in the kitchen.

I turned from the window, for a moment blinded by a sudden slanting ferocity of October sun. A man stood blocking the kitchen doorway. It was Ben. And he could not speak. I grabbed him. I shook him. I pushed him against the door. Useless to ask, "What happened?" To ask, "What is it?" A face contorted in fear and agony almost obliterates the need for words.

Then a name. "Stephen ... in the lake," he gasped. "Asthma ... attack." I stopped for a second. Not William. Oh, God ... in whom I do not believe ... thank God.

I am not a monster. With Elizabeth's cries of, "Oh, no. No," I ran to try to save her child.

I ran across the lawn, through the garden, on and on through the park and then down to the lake.

But someone had got there before me. William. My son. Trying desperately to save Stephen.

From the top of the hill I saw them. Together in the water. They seemed to rise slowly. Gracefully. Like dancers. As though some great force propelled them through the surface of the water. Towards the sky.

Stephen seemed to hug William to him. Like a lover. Unwilling to let go. Fierce in possession. Winning. They went down. And the muddy lake closed over them. How many times?

How many times had the lake closed over them? "Save yourself, William" screamed out of me.

And "Let him go" carried on the wind. Into nothing. The muddy lake closed over them. Again.

And still I ran, Elizabeth after me, down the long hill. I fell into the water, and I swam to where it seemed to me they had gone down. I dived. Into black nothing. And murkiness. Why not blue waters clear for them?

I dived again. And again. And again, nothing. Filth. Sediment. And darkness. And now pain. Physical pain. Something to fill me up. I came to the surface. And down again. And again. Over and over again. But I could not find their secret place. Elizabeth, far away from me, was frantically swimming around. Diving over and over again.

We swam towards the bank. And fell on it.

She held her arms out to me. Love and pity. Defeating me again.

"Damn you, Elizabeth. Stephen brought him down. I know it. Stephen brought him down. My William. Trying to save him. Stephen brought him down. Oh, God. Oh, God."

Why should I call on You now?

"Oh, God. How I hate you, Elizabeth. My God, Elizabeth. You're done for me at last."

I moved towards her. And I spat water over her. Then I took stones. I threw them at her. I made my hand a weapon. The palm held sideways—like a knife—and I hit her jaw. I moved towards her neck. I moved, ready to kill. Then I saw a dead bird on the ground. I picked it up. And splattered it onto her chest.

She lay there weeping and whispered, "Ruth. Don't. Think of our boys. Our boys."

And I stopped at last. And looked down at her. Was something broken? I could not see through the blood. Whether I got to the bone or whether—again—I had only hurt soft tissue. The smell? That could have been the rotting body of the bird. Parts of which clung to her dress. And not something rotten in Elizabeth that I had at last burst open. Not exquisitely, as I had dreamed, but with sick, defeated, ferocious grief.

Then, racing down the hill came the ambulance men. Carrying their useless stretchers. I ran towards them, screaming.

"They're at the bottom of the lake. I can't get

them. The stretcher's useless. There is no body."
Stephen's face floated into my consciousness.
"There are no bodies."

They stood helpless. The willing helpers. Those
trained to deal with dramatic death. They looked
lost without a body. Carefully to move and place
onto their precious canvas altar.

"The fire brigade ... their divers are on their
way." A young woman in a suit spoke.

"Mrs. Garton?"

"Who are you?" I almost spat the words at this
intruder.

"I'm Sarah Duncan and ... this must be ..."
She turned towards Elizabeth.

"Elizabeth Harding, I'm Stephen's mother."

"The ... phone call said ... two boys. ..."

"Stephen and William."

"Your sons?"

"Yes."

"I am so ... so ..."

Sorry?

"Mrs. Garton. If we went to the house it would
be ... better."

"No."

"Mrs. Garton ... please."

"No."

"Lady Harding?"

Elizabeth shook her head. Blood dripped down
and mixed itself with some particles of flesh from
the bird. And Elizabeth's shirt was blue. Not white

as normal. I had not noticed this before. The doctor bent down and from her case took gauze and tinctures. And started to repair some of the damage I had done to Elizabeth's face.

"I fell," she said. "Badly. Running towards the . . . boys. Onto the bird. And I fell onto the edge of the lake when I was getting out."

I said nothing. Someone had handed me a large blanket to wrap around my shoulders.

"Mrs. Garton. Lady Harding. It would be better for you to remove your wet clothes."

"No." From us both.

Healers hate to feel useless. Hate to recognise that nothing works. Like priests, they need to prove their power. Most particularly in extremis. Except that, unlike priests, they have nothing to offer the dead body. Certainly not what the priest can offer—a new disembodied existence. Still with us. But not seen. Why should the dead want to stay? Watching the weeping but not able to join in. After all, it was their life that was lost. No future. Time finished for them. Full stop. No new sentence. No new paragraph.

The boys' lives. A short story. Their future, gone. No future. "Never, never, never, never, never." Five nevers. I always thought that significant. And "kill, kill, kill, kill, kill, kill." Lear needed the six beats for his rage. The two interwoven, of course. For who has grieved who has not raged? And raged, again.

And now, along the top of the hill, ran dark figures. Rubber-armoured. For the water. Their heads encased in monstrous balaclavas for the deep.

I swam with them to the point of my last vision of my son. As he left me. Another clasped too tightly to him. How mothers hate all others who embrace their child too tightly. They know how easy it is to squeeze life away. So that only a body remains.

And the remains of his life, this body which I had so loved, came finally to the surface. Attached to the other. The boys' legs, like tree trunks, were wrapped around each other. Like lovers in sleep. Motionless. Stephen's arms locked round William's waist. William's face seemed pressed deeply into Stephen's chest. As though it were a part of Stephen's body. Stephen's head was thrown back. His last act had been to gasp for air. Before he brought William down. How well Stephen had known all his life what it was to gasp for air.

And suddenly it was what I had to do. Not to cry. Just suddenly, convulsively, to gasp for air. I lived.

Dead bodies are heavy. The young divers, like warriors in a field of battle, tried to prise the boys apart.

"No."

"No?"

"No."

"Mrs. Garton . . ."

"Leave them as they are. Don't separate them."

"But . . ."

"Don't separate them."

The bodies—like a single statue—were laid on the bank. It seemed a single death. So much did they resemble a sculpture of one long, fine young man. His head that of Stephen. And his legs those of William.

The men began their work. Two of them gently releasing the bodies as the others forced oxygen into their rejecting lungs. Trying, these strangers, to deceive death.

But death had been clever. With one's weakness, and the other's love, death had harvested them both. And the sun still shone, in a weak October way. It did not withdraw in sorrow. Not even when death's triumph was finally acknowledged.

Lexington waited for us and our entourage, as we walked slowly towards it with our dead children. The boys. Our sons. Who after all would not now have the east or west wing. Perhaps Lexington rejoiced, that in time it might be left alone at last.

Through the French windows and onto the terrace ran Charles and Dominick. My mother stood motionless, eyes closed.

"Oh, my God. . . . Oh, my God." Dominick's voice.

He did not run to me. He turned, retching into the protection of the half hedge that separated the terrace from the lawn. Charles stood looking down at the stretchers, guarded on either side by Elizabeth and me, standing behind the bearers. He covered his face for a moment. Then he turned and removed my mother from the path of the carriers with their heavy burden.

At the front of the house, the waiting ambulance received its cargo. We followed slowly in cars. Not ready yet for a longer separation. The young policeman stayed with Ben to take his statement.

At the little village hospital, questions were asked of us by the gentlest of police sergeants, and the most solicitous of doctors. As though, in searching for the answer to how, we could find the answer to why.

At some stage, by unspoken consent, we drove through the dusk back to Lexington. A Lexington we could no longer recognise. It had tricked us. Made us feel safe all those years. In my soft weaving of hatred, I had never felt afraid. Had I defiled Lexington? No. No. Elizabeth's son had killed mine.

I bore no guilt. Not in this. I do not—will not accept another interpretation. For that way madness lies.

Twenty-six

It is pointless to describe the next few days. Those who know, know. Those who don't, will never understand.

The Funeral. And boys came from their school to represent the pupils. With their sturdy legs, they burned my eyes. With their faces, they poured vinegar down my throat. And with their sweet voices, they poisoned my ears.

A sad headmaster and solemn teachers now gave life reports on the boys, whose time they had expected to measure out in terms.

A government minister, and figures from the world of affairs, and people from the worlds of arts and publishing and academia mingled uneasily together. No one knew what to say. Because the words did not exist.

Lexington gathered them in, and impressed them. And fed them—after we had laid the boys, now separated, in their graves, side by side in the village churchyard, beside my family. My grave child, William. Now most truly a grave child. He should never have been mine. Too good for me. Was there a pattern here? Some scheme to destroy me. If any of my family had been any good . . . couldn't they have interceded on our behalf? Then I remembered. I did not believe in God. Or in the afterlife. And I found that comforting.

Twenty-seven

How old and lined we looked on the following morning. But there was no respite. Death demands a new life. No settling into the same old rut after death. It has a double triumph. It robs life, and fatally stings those remaining. What power.

Now, it used the weakest member, Dominick, to shake us out of any illusion of peace. With harmony forever gone from his life, he wanted to be "straight" with me . . . with us all . . . for the first time in years.

Straight, Dominick? A line, perhaps. Part of something. A rectangle? No, a triangle. Or perhaps not. There were four of us, after all.

"Did you know, Elizabeth . . . that Charles had an affair with Ruth?"

She sat so quietly, without moving at all, that I thought she had not heard.

"Elizabeth. I'm talking to you. Did you know?"

"No."

"What are you doing, Dominick?"

"I'm revealing a truth. After all, we've just experienced the ultimate truth. Makes all this look rather pathetic."

"Then why do it?"

"I need . . . I need this, Ruth. I need this. I have more courage now."

Courage? God!

"I guessed a little time ago it was Charles. Before . . . this . . . I felt that I would die without you, Ruth. But, then, I knew nothing of pain. Three days ago, I knew nothing. I don't want whatever's left to be a lie. It's extraordinary how desperately I want something in my life that is . . . real."

"What Dominick has told you is true, Elizabeth."

"Thank you for that, at least, Charles." Then turning to Dominick: "It's amazing how many people we bring down with the truth."

"I'm sorry. I have to do this. In the end, everybody tries to save his own life."

"Not quite everybody, Dominick. William didn't." I remembered my last vision of him.

"He did a brave thing. And lost," Charles said.

"Well, I wish to God he hadn't been brave. I wish to God he'd saved himself."

"So do I, Ruth. So do I. To lose Stephen, and know his asthma brought about William's death . . . is agony." Elizabeth started to cry. We were all silent.

Then she began to speak. Quietly. "How the world has turned. Everything is broken here. In Lexington. In this house, where I've been so quiet. All my life I've been quiet. So quiet. For I knew . . . since I was very small, that this was not really my place. I was here . . . because of a death. I had inherited a grief. But I was loved. So loved. But still I never had the confidence . . . to be . . . difficult. Or to displease.

"And when Ruth was born, it seemed even more important. The more she became Ruth—Ruth the wild, Ruth the dangerous, the brilliant—the more I needed to be good and quiet. That was me. Elizabeth—the good one. It's a way of life now. A habit was formed. I don't know another way to be. No courage, you see. Not for Dominick's cruelty, even now. And I don't know how to deceive—as you've done, Charles. And you, Ruth. I lack the . . . the stamina . . . yes. I lack the stamina to do what you have done."

"I love you, Elizabeth. Please, please, understand that . . . please." Charles moved towards her, beseeching her. I watched him. Beseeching her.

Tell him, Elizabeth. Tell him how I attacked you. Tell him.

"Charles . . . dear Charles. Don't. Some instinct tells me we must not continue. Perhaps you're for Ruth, and not for me. I had something perfect once, with Hubert. Maybe, if he'd lived, it would have become less perfect. But I don't think so. No. No. I'm certain. So I'll just take that memory . . . if I may. May I . . . Ruth?"

"What do you mean?"

"Oh, Hubert, forgive me. Please forgive me." She cried to him. After all those years.

"Hubert is . . . was yours, and only yours."

"I know that, Ruth. I don't need your affirmation."

"Stop all this. Elizabeth. Please, Elizabeth. I do not want this." Charles gripped the edge of the table. As though he needed support.

"Charles. Neither do I. But I must do it."

All of us looked at her. And knew that she would. For, in the end, there is something stony in the heart of goodness. Which is perhaps why, all too often, we avoid it.

Later, the inquest, investigation of Death. Pointless. For Death always commits the perfect murder. He has never been caught. He uses so many disguises. The face of illness. Or accident. Or violence. The list is endless. He is cruel, funny, macabre, wild, gentle. He is secret. Famous. He hides. Then leaps into full view. He is magnificent. Pathetic. Bathetic. But always, always, Death is triumphant.

Facts. Established by questions. And answers. Asthma attack. Stephen's. A non-swimmer. Ben. A hero. William. Racing on his bicycle to save Stephen, floundering desperately . . . his asthma choking him . . . in the water. William, a hero, who failed. Two deaths. Too early. There were questions I did not want to hear. To which I gave answers. But did not truly speak.

After the inquest, she left.

In Charles's eyes I became Judas Iscariot. That night, he too left Lexington. And I rent my garments.

Months later he came back. Weakness, I suppose. Elizabeth was adamant. Utterly impervious to all his pleas. She had gone to live in a remote part of Scotland. In a cottage outside a small village. To paint. Ridiculous, to me, that so small a talent could sustain her.

I took him gratefully. For I knew that he loved me to the limits of which he was capable. It was not his fault that I had gone further. And found myself alone. I had found that I longed for him . . . continuously. And I decided to be true to something. The longing was real enough. It seemed then, and still does, sufficient.

Twenty-eight

We live in Lexington now. We sold the studio flat in London. My home with Dominick. And William.

Elizabeth's studio is rented. For a nominal sum. To a young artist, Beatrice, I forget her second name, who had . . . a look about her. We never visit. All financial matters are handled through an agent.

Charles has given Frimton to his son, Christopher. He returned to England. A married man. With a young family. Two boys. I do not visit.

I came back to Lexington, for my mother. A sudden kindness. Or was it penance? Elizabeth had said goodbye to her. Extraordinary, her late cruelty. But my mother will not hear a word against her, and always says, "I understand." So do I—in a way. But it is a long road from understanding to acceptance. And I haven't even begun the journey.

There is no question of divorce from Elizabeth. Irrelevant, Charles says. She says nothing. To my knowledge. So we live in Lexington, this man and I. The bodies work together. Still move together— in a manner perhaps programmed in us before we were born. Afterwards, he turns from me. Still. In his sorrow. And his pleasure.

Drugged, in a way, we continue. The surface of our lives is tense. But we're familiar with that now, and it is less distressing than might be supposed.

When he looks at me with hatred, as he sometimes does, I accept the blow. And when my nakedness offends him, I cover myself. There was a time when I was a goddess.

Where once I searched for clues to understand her, now I have all I need to study her. Pictures. Letters. Clothes. Perfumes. Soaps. Books.

And her husband.

And still I do not know her.

When Charles is away—less often now—I sit in her room. I look in the mirror, and I use her small array of beauty aids. I bought a blonde wig. Metamorphosis.

Sometimes I wear her clothes and her face and hair for hours. Gazing endlessly into the mirror, I remember a teacher at school who had warned of the devil who looks back—if you gaze too long at yourself. The devil does not look back at me. But then, would I recognise him? Elizabeth does not gaze back at me, however closely and falsely I resemble her. And Ruth does not gaze back either. For I am neither Ruth nor Elizabeth. Just a reflection. Bits of me. And bits of her.

I never thought to lay this mutant out for Charles. I feared he would have seen the horror of it. And might have killed it.

But my creation, like Frankenstein's, discovered a life of its own. Once, when I believed Charles was away, as I did my essential, daily penitential walks around the lake, once for William, once for Stephen, he . . . encountered it.

And weeping fell upon it.

All was different. The movements. The sighs. The rhythm.

Afterwards, I felt I knew her better.

As he walked in silence towards Lexington, I left the golden hair and blue jeans and white shirt on the bank. And, wet before I ever touched the water, swam through the bitter April waves to the other side and back again.

There were visions of course. Of the human adolescent statue. But I knew it well.

I still have my own times. When I am magnificent, voluptuous. When I—Ruth—rise and fall on sheets or on the ground for him.

But less often. I feel no resentment.

Dominick? Well, Dominick left. Not quietly either. With as much anger and bitterness as his exhausted soul could muster. I do not blame him. He went to California. Back into academic life. He is much feted. Perhaps you've heard of him? There was a brief period of intense promiscuity. He wrote to me—about this aspect of his new life. I burned the letter. In case he has another child. In his new life.

A few years ago he married a tall, blonde, brainy cliché—fifteen years his junior. I smile sometimes to think of it. He is adored, I gather, as once he adored. A proper harmony. Balance achieved at last.

No doubt he has a tale he tells. Tales of me. And who knows. He may be telling the truth.

Twenty-nine

I am an excellent driver. I drive fast, with intense concentration. I disdain automatic models, believing that an essential rhythm is lost. Charles, now more deeply involved in his charity work, had to attend, as a member of an advisory committee, a weeklong EC investigation into the rights of refugees.

I chose this week to drive to Scotland to see Elizabeth. I had to see her. The memory was fading. After two years. My own disguise as Elizabeth was no longer satisfactory.

Although I was certain that Charles had her address, it was unseemly, I felt, to ask him. After some lies and subterfuge, I got it through the gallery, which was having increasing success with her painting. She was now taken more seriously by everyone. Her tragedy enhanced her reputation. And living alone in Scotland also rather added to it. As did her consistent refusal to be interviewed. It's not enough to produce the work. Very important also to live the life prescribed for the artist. Loneliness. Suffering, if possible. And poverty. Elizabeth remained deeply disappointing in this last respect.

I risked her anger. And Charles's. Would she tell him? I hoped that enough of the old Elizabeth remained to make that unlikely. I had to do it. Perhaps I would just look at the cottage. I was desperate for a physical background against which I could place her current life. In my thoughts, for I thought of her daily. Hourly perhaps. An old obsession.

I arrived at twilight. Her cottage was three miles outside a small village, dominated by a grand sweep of mountain. A vast playground for the light, racing against the clouds as if to see who would win. Good spot for Elizabeth the artist. Beautiful and obvious.

I believe in surprise. I simply drove unannounced to the front of the cottage. There were low windows on either side of the wooden door. I knocked. After a few minutes, standing there in the silence, I tried to look in through a window.

"Yes?"

I turned. Embarrassed. Caught in an act of . . .

peeping? What an ugly word. A tall young man in his early twenties stood in the doorway.

"Is Elizabeth here?"

"Who are you?"

"Her . . . sister." Well said, Ruth.

"She doesn't have a sister."

"Really? Who are you?"

"I don't have to answer that."

"Full of charm, aren't you? Where's Elizabeth?"

"Not here."

"Will she be coming back?" I suppose detective work is like this. I would probably have been good at it.

"I don't know."

"Now, listen. I clearly must look extremely threatening to you. A strange five-foot-eight female confronting your six-foot-two muscular frame. It's possible I'm intent on robbery. Even rape. I fully sympathise with your terror at my arrival. But I am Elizabeth Ashbridge's sister. My name is Ruth Garton. I would like to come in and wait for her. I do not expect tea or wine and certainly not a welcome from you. May I?" I walked towards the door.

"No. You may not."

"Let's start again. How do you do?"

"How do you do?" He repeated the words.

"You're not English?"

"Certainly not."

"Good accent, though."

151

"Gee, thanks."

"Where did you polish what I assume was once a drawl?"

"In London."

"Doing what?"

"Studying."

"What?"

"Art."

"Aha. Where?"

"St. Martin's."

"Really. I'm impressed. So. You love Elizabeth's work. Decided to come and worship the artist?"

"Yes and no."

"No? Let's deal with the no first."

"Do you always do that? Deal with the no first."

"Yes. Saves time."

"I'd never heard of Elizabeth. I was on a walking holiday—came into this valley and saw her. Standing in the river, thigh-high waders . . ." He paused for a second. "But I do admire her work. Though not deeply."

Well, that's a start.

"And yes?"

"I worship Elizabeth."

He said it so suddenly, so sweetly, that, for a second, emotion cut into the repartee, wounding it slightly.

"Worship her?"

"Yes."

152

He smiled slowly. Sexily. "What did you say your name was?"

"Ruth."

"Well, Ruth, I think you should turn and leave now."

"Why?"

"Because you have an air about you. I recognise it."

"What kind of air?"

"Oh. I don't know. Something disturbing. Nothing very major. I don't like your style. I don't like the way you speak."

"Ah, Elizabeth must have spoken of me then. About my style?"

"Elizabeth has never mentioned you. I can just sense it."

"Which sense?"

"What?"

"Which sense? Sight? Smell? It can't be touch?"

"You never change, do you, Ruth?"

On the skin of my back, her voice seemed to beat out the words. I turned to look at her. My face felt frozen. I could not rearrange it.

Oh, I change, Elizabeth. All the time. Sometimes, Elizabeth, sometimes, I am you. But I'm losing touch. And I need to study you again.

And I did. She was still recognisably herself. Body still thin, tall. A creamy sweater over white shirt. The jeans. Heavy Wellington boots instead of loafers. Beaten, weathered almost, but still her-self.

"Well, Daniel. You did your best . . . but Ruth is . . ."

I waited for a clue to myself. From her.

"I've been expecting you in a way. I suppose you must do this."

"I suppose I must."

"Well then. Come in. Fill your eyes."

"Elizabeth! That sounded a little bit like me. Al-most mocking."

She shook her head in disbelief.

I entered. It was a long, low white room. Large stone fireplace. Logs, of course. A heavy wooden table, off-centre. Grey armchairs scattered around, covered in paisley shawls. All as one would have expected. Running along the entire back wall of the house was a kind of verandah, with a high glass roof, a stone back wall, a heavy door. A stu-dio, I suppose. For her.

I filled my eyes.

"I'd love some wine."

Elizabeth sighed.

"Red?"

The boy . . . what was his name? Daniel . . . yes. Daniel took a bottle from the cupboard and poured us all a glass of Burgundy. At least he drinks.

Stop it, Ruth. I killed the vision of William as the young man he never grew to be. Stop it.

"Elizabeth, you never mentioned me?"

"No."

"Does he know nothing?"

"Nothing."

"How extraordinary. But then it's all extraordinary."

"Yes, it is. Daniel, Ruth is . . . absorbing you. Be careful."

Had she lost a kind of innocence? Perhaps the good should always arm themselves. Against an excess of innocence.

He smiled.

"Well, why did you come?" he asked.

"To see Elizabeth. That's all."

"Ruth and I share ghosts," Elizabeth explained. "And a knowledge. Which no one else could ever understand. Even I don't understand it very well. Even after . . ."

"It's a very strong bond, Daniel. I hope you never find out."

"Can't you defeat them? The ghosts?"

"Oh, no. It's they who have defeated us. We're like wounded soldiers. On a battlefield they have deserted."

"Deserted? They left willingly?"

"We'll never know. Last moments. What goes on in the mind in last moments? No more questions?" I turned to Daniel.

"No."

"Why so reticent?"

"Why not? It's a habit."

155

"You're very young to have such . . . discipline."

"It's not discipline."

"What then?"

"Love."

I looked away. Elizabeth sat down, in a large armchair close to the light. She laid her head back, and spoke quietly. "You know, Ruth, it's useless to fight you. Do you understand that was why I decided to love you instead?"

"No. Decided to?"

"It wasn't natural. I told you this before. I think I guessed, early on, that to fight you might be dangerous. Might enrage you further."

"Enrage me?"

"Yes. You were full of hidden angers. Against me."

"You never said anything."

"What could I have said? I hoped, in time, that if I was quiet and careful with you . . . I tried to be separate from you. But you were always there on the edges . . . in the background."

"I didn't think you noticed."

"You were wrong. It didn't seem to matter. Then . . . with Hubert. Well, we almost made a life together, in France. Ah. But that's a life I never got to live. I sometimes live it, you know . . . in dreams. A parallel life. In a dream. Like I dream of the boys. Still."

"Yes. I know that dreamworld too."

I looked at Daniel, sitting so calmly, opposite Elizabeth.

"Elizabeth. You haven't asked about Charles."

"Who is Charles?" Daniel turned to Elizabeth.

"My husband," she replied.

"Ah."

"He lives with Ruth now." She paused.

"Is he . . . the man? The one who comes?"

She passed a hand across her mouth, as though she had been the one to pose the painful question.

"Charles comes here? Does Charles come here? I must know."

"Must you? Ruth, that's so very like you . . . that 'must.' And with it goes your belief that I will answer. Why?"

"Because you are . . . you're Elizabeth."

"Yes. And you always expect a certain behaviour from me. I've flirted with . . . I've flirted with your way. But I'm set in my own."

I realised her strength again. Why she would linger forever in people's lives. And why the loss of her was hard.

"Charles comes to visit me once a year. It's a private thing."

Daniel stood up and moved towards Elizabeth.

"I didn't know he was your husband."

"You've met?" I turned incredulously to him.

"No. I saw him once. Through the window. I came back . . . too early. I had agreed with Elizabeth to leave them alone. I didn't know who he was."

"What did you see?"

There was a short silence.

"A man kneeling in front of a woman."

As once my father knelt to her.

"She stroked his head. And pressed him to her stomach. They stayed like that for . . . oh, maybe half an hour. And then he left."

I knew, of course. But had preferred not to. The past . . . in this . . . had not been so unpredictable.

"Charles talked about me? To you?"

"Not really. But I know. I . . . I know he feels . . . most deeply."

"How can you know?"

"I know."

"Why did you leave him?"

Silence.

"Why did you let me have him?"

Silence.

"Because, Ruth . . . he is yours. And I had had my day."

"What do you mean?"

"Hubert. Hubert was true. To me, and to his promise. Charles tried. But he . . . he failed. I'm harsh in this, I think."

"And Daniel?"

"There are no promises between Daniel and me."

"I'd give you a promise. And keep it. If you'd let me."

"But I won't let you, Daniel."

He looked at me as though to read my thoughts.

"You're thinking bodies, aren't you, Ruth? I'm young, and Elizabeth's not. And young girls' bodies. And why am I not with them? Bodies. You're thinking bodies, Ruth."

"I'm not quite as banal as you seem to imagine."

"Perhaps not. Well, let me tell you about bodies. From my experience. I lived in California. I had my first 'crush' on a girl when I was fifteen. She was beautiful. She was tall with long, blond hair. Her waist tapered. It tapered into a kind of chalice. Small hipbones, and skin stretched tight across her stomach and creamy blonde pubic hair. I painted her. With what my teachers used to call my 'high eye.' I suppose she was my first model. I worshipped her body every day, I knew I would feel like that forever. But then I met Oona.

"Oona had short, thick, black hair. She wasn't tall. Her breasts were out of proportion to everything else. I couldn't get them out of my mind. Until Catherine."

He ran his hand through his hair. And smiled at us. He was . . . young.

"Catherine was an athlete. Half French. Brown eyes, black hair, and her body just worked. You know, everything just seemed to fit together. Nothing out of alignment. She used to laugh a lot.

That's all I can remember about her. But the body, I remember . . . perfectly. From the time I was fifteen I've had bodies . . . girls' bodies. Bodies, I know about. Body sex. Great rush of crazy pleasure."

"And then?"

"And then you get greedy."

"For what?"

"For more. By that stage the bodies aren't enough. Now you want mind games. Games of power. Rejection. False jealousy. Eventually, even adolescents need an aphrodisiac."

I was becoming tired. The vision of Charles, suppliant before her, was agonising.

"No matter what Daniel says, he'll leave someday."

"Is that what you long for, Ruth? Another loss for me? What will satisfy you? My death, perhaps?"

Perhaps.

"You're like a child, Ruth. What you can't have, you must destroy. That habit of destructiveness has spoiled everything you had, and have. You'll spoil what you have with Charles. Because of your anger at his small need of me. You want that as well."

She looked at me with love and pity. And her obstinate, stubborn goodness shone out.

My old hatred of her leapt like a hound to my mouth. And I wanted to sting her with my tears.

Again. And watch her weep for her Hubert. Again. And see her sadness as she left Charles. Again. Let the hound tear her for the agony that would never leave me—the day her child drowned mine.

If I could kill you, Elizabeth, I would. I would. If I could only choose the way. If I could strangle you, I would. If I could plunge a knife into you, I would. If I could shoot you, I would shoot you through the eyes. And I would look on you, and be released. At last.

Terrible things started to happen to my body. In my head, sounds, like high-pitched screams, made it impossible for me to hear what she was mouthing. Red mist obscured the face of Daniel, which seemed to float in shock close to mine. And my mouth was full of something . . . venom . . . venomous . . . I ran screaming down the corridor of myself. Looking for a last door. There was some other force shaking my body. My bones were becoming liquid. Elizabeth and Daniel tried to catch the liquid as it spilled on the floor. I was being torn asunder. I had miscarried myself. The red became black. And Stephen and William were drowning again. The second time for them. Oh, what cruelty. To make them swallow the water again. Oh, boys. Both boys. They cried out. "Not again. Not again." Were they drowning in my liquid body? Could someone scoop it up and make a thing of it? Was there a vessel to contain me? Something to hold me together? Words, more words came, and drowned the screams inside my head. I cannot, will not speak them. "I bear no guilt." These are the only words I will speak.

Other words, other words were beating their way to the surface. Stop the words, Ruth. In terror, I spat my venom in her face. I raised my arm, no longer liquid, to strike her. I needed a weapon. I picked a knife from the table. I saw her eyes . . . and all the pain. And all the love. And all the goodness. And turned the blade upon myself. Of course. And at last.

The boy was suddenly behind me. Disarming me. Trapping me with his arms. We fell awkwardly, obscenely round the room, as he grappled for control. Finally he pinned me underneath him. And I was quiet at last.

He—this boy—was holding my insanity down. The heat of his stomach pressed into mine. The length of his legs held my lower limbs. His arms pinned mine into subjugation. His hands stroked my face, and he whispered, "It's all right. You're all right. It's OK. It's OK."

Little words. Nothing words. Were they words of absolution for me? "It's all right. It's OK. It's OK." Such little words.

And he almost smiled at me. Her son-boy.

Then he released me step by step. Legs. Arms. His hands slid from my face. Finally, he rolled off my chest and stomach. Certain that the beast was tamed. My clothes were soiled with my vomit.

My urine. I looked at Daniel and Elizabeth. They showed no disgust.

They walked me to the bathroom. Both of them helped me into the bath. My nakedness was nothing to me or to them. I climbed into their bed. They lay on either side of me until I slept.

When I awoke it was late morning. A little carriage clock showed eleven-thirty. The door opened, and Elizabeth brought tea, and toast and honey. She sat in silence as I ate. A loving silence. Which I could feel. From which I did not recoil. She gave me her clothes. Oh, the irony. She had put mine in a little bag. I dressed in her jeans, which I rolled up, and her heavy sweater, which came almost to my knees. Dressed in Elizabeth's clothes, by Elizabeth.

Later, I felt that I watched myself leave them. We all knew I could. And that I was ready.

I saw them in the car mirror as they turned to walk back towards the house. A tall young man, and a long-limbed woman. Impossible to tell her age from the back.

And I knew that they had saved my life.

Thirty

I never told Charles of my visit. A fact. Though sometimes he looked at me and said, "You've changed, Ruth. You seem a little more at peace." And so I was. A little.

Elizabeth sent the boy away soon afterwards.

How did I know?

He came to Lexington. Silent. Pale. No, white. I opened the door. He just shook his head. Slowly. Again and again. His pain enraged me. I was still not as I ought to be. The years of malice were not undone. I did not help him. I felt unworthy, you see.

That is a lie.

I was afraid that Charles would see him. Oh,

shame on me. My face contorted. I felt its muscles move to lock him out.

To force his pain back onto him. To crush him. He took the blow. He bowed his head. Then he walked away.

"Who is it?" Charles called.

By the time Charles came to the door, the boy had vanished.

"It was no one," I said.

I never heard from him again.

Thirty-one

All this happened some years ago. The number is irrelevant.

She is dead now.

She died from cancer. I had a phone call from a local doctor. Apparently she had named me as the next of kin.

"Mrs. Garton?"

"Yes."

"I'm Dr. Mackintosh."

"Yes."

"I'm afraid I have some . . . sad news . . . about Elizabeth Ashbridge."

"Is she dead?"

"Yes. I'm sorry."

"How?"

"Cancer. It was very quick. Breast cancer. Started in the left breast. I am afraid she came too late. She was an extraordinary woman."

"Yes, I know."

"When I told her about the cancer she said, 'How strange that it didn't grow in the heart.' I'll never forget that. 'How strange it didn't grow in the heart.' She said it was grief, you see."

"Perhaps it was."

"I believe you're her closest relative. You're her sister?"

"In a way."

"I don't know what more to say. Will you . . . ?"

"Yes. Let me take your address. And the hospital address. We . . . er . . . Charles and I, will take care of everything. We'll be with you this evening."

"I look forward to meeting you. I have some . . . instructions . . . which Mrs. Ashbridge wanted to give you. In the event of her death, that is. They concern her burial I believe. She didn't show me the letter, you understand."

"I see. Naturally, we'll do as Elizabeth asked."

"Yes. Of course."

"I must speak to my mother. To her mother. I'm so grateful. Thank you."

I put the phone down.

My life's . . . my life's companion . . . was gone. She had died in the night. As I lay beside Charles. We had felt nothing. We had simply slept through her death. Will I sleep through Charles's? Or will he sleep through mine? And then sleep afterwards? I have slept since the boys died.

Charles was in the garden. I walked up to him and stood behind him for a second. Silent. Then I said the words. He turned to me. No tears. Nothing.

"She left me a long time ago, Ruth. It was then I learned how . . . bitter life could be."

"We should go, I think. Together. To bring her home."

"Yes."

"Who else . . . to tell?"

"Mother. And the Baathus family."

"Yes. Yes, of course."

Would they have a clear memory of her? Their son's wife? Who had outlived him. Till now.

"Yes. I'll phone them."

"So. Let's go then, together."

And we did.

We did not bring her home. We buried her in the local churchyard. As instructed. Her letter to us was short. A note really. It said:

"Not beside the boys. I know you will understand. Here. A simple cross with my name. Nothing else."

We followed her instructions. Almost. We put ELIZABETH ASHBRIDGE. ARTIST on the tombstone. A white marble cross.

There was a brief reading of the will. She left everything to me. There were a number of obituaries in the papers. Short, not very enlightening. No one knew her.

Charles and I beat out our time quietly now. We mark anniversaries where once we marked birthdays.

And if I'd never met her, would I have been good?

For in the end, that's all that matters.

We are here to add to the sum of human goodness. To prove the thing exists. And however futile each individual act of courage or generosity, self-sacrifice or grace—it still proves the thing exists. Each act adds to the fund. It needs replenishment. Not only because evil flourishes, and is, most indefensibly, defended. But because goodness is no longer a respectable aim in life. The hound of hell, envy, has driven it from the house.

We two, Charles and I, once united by the powerful bond of sin, now float towards each other across a sea of sorrow. Above the faces of the boys, who rise and fall, to watery graves, again and again.

And as we move towards each other, the face of Elizabeth also rises. Again and again.

And if I had never met her? What then? Did she create me? Or I her? Did I dream her? Am I Elizabeth? Now?

These questions long engage me. Do you have answers? Please. Please, answer me.

Answer me, as I leave you now.

As I leave you.

As I leave.